EPIC!
*– Match of the Day Magazine*

"I love the way that they are about so much more
an football: they are about heart, values and family.
h graphic novel and fiction titles are compelling,
aging and a lot of fun. Lace up and get reading."

n Sells, Programme manager for Sport & Literacy,
National Literacy Trust

as everything that today's children need as they
w up. It is jam-packed with positive role models,
involvement in Women's Football, respect, mental
eing, good work ethic, education and aspiration."
*– Books for Topics*

cks a lot of punch in its short and simple to read
jes... It captures the feel of playing and having a
passion for football at an early age very well."
*– Comic Scene Magazine*

"I give it 5,000,000 stars. Amazing!"
*– The Book Brothers*

"I kr w already that it will be a popular title amongst
ur football-loving children (not just boys!)."
*– That Boy Can Teach*

First published 2022 by Rebellion Publishing Ltd,
Riverside House, Osney Mead, Oxford, OX2 0ES, UK

ISBN: 978 1 78618 495 5

10 9 8 7 6 5 4 3 2 1

A CIP catalogue record for this book is available
from the British Library.

Printed in Denmark

Creative Director and CEO: Jason Kingsley
Chief Technical Officer: Chris Kingsley
Head of Publishing: Ben Smith
Publishing Manager: Beth Lewis
Editors: Olivia Hicks & Amy Borsuk
Design: Sam Gretton
Cover image: Elkys Nova
PR & Marketing Manager: Jamie Elby

**Follow us:**

 royoftheroversofficial  royoftheroversofficial  royoftherovers

www.royoftherovers.com   info@royoftherovers.com

## ALSO IN THIS SERIES

Illustrated fiction by Tom Palmer:

*Scouted*
*Team Work*
*Play-Offs*
*On Tour*
*From The Ashes*
*Rocky*
*Sudden Death*

Graphic novels by Rob Williams,
Ben Willsher, Lisa Henke & David Sque:

*Kick-Off*
*Foul Play*
*Going Up*
*Transferred*
*All To Play For*
*Pressure*
*New Digs*

For Iris

ROCKY HAD NEVER been on an aeroplane before. It was something she had wanted to do for years, watching them fly high over the city, their vapour trails pointing to exciting destinations far away from Melchester.

The closest she had been was a day out with Mum, Dad and Roy at the side of terminal two at Melchester Airport, where Mum paid a fiver each for them all to watch planes land and take off on a runway that was at least half a mile away from where they were sitting eating cheese sandwiches.

It had been fun, exciting, thrilling. But nothing like being inside an aeroplane.

Now here she was. Airborne.

Rocky Race flying at thirty-five thousand feet above continental Europe. Another of her dreams had come true. Although it wasn't exactly what she had expected. But things never were, were they? Rocky was coming to understand that.

At the airport, while waiting for their gate to be announced, Rocky and her teammates, Priscilla Danquah and Helena Pielichaty – all wearing Melchester Rovers tracksuits – watched a YouTube film called 'The World's Most Frightening Airplane Landings', a collection of terrifying near-miss air disasters. While watching the fun, they had been drinking coffee, eating cake and generally winding each other up with the idea that their own flight might end up on a disaster video. They laughed hysterically, goading each other to watch more and more scary films of planes coming off the end of runways, wheels exploding on landing and wings touching the ground, while the other members of Melchester Rovers FC trawled the duty free shops, searching for bargain sportswear, or were just sitting calmly listening to music on their headphones.

In the air, high above the world, Rocky was starting to regret watching those videos. Maybe the coffees too. She'd been able to cope with take-off. And with being in the sky in a tiny tube of metal. That all felt okay, fun, exciting. But landing? She was less at ease with that. What was it like when you had to slow down and hit the ground?

As the plane descended through the clouds, the passengers bumping about, light flickering from dark to bright, threads of water streaming horizontally across the oval fuselage windows, Rocky looked at Helena, then Priscilla. And all those YouTube images of what could go wrong in the next two minutes came back to her.

Helena – tall with straight light hair tied back in a ponytail and the kindest smile – claimed that she couldn't even remember how many planes she'd been on in her life. She had been born in Sweden and her mum and dad were from Poland and Ukraine, but had lived in the UK most of her life. It meant that she'd travelled a lot. Flown a lot.

Priscilla was the same. She had family in Canada and the Caribbean and had flown on long haul flights since she was a kid.

Rocky was sort of in awe of Helena and Priscilla. They had such interesting backgrounds. Both with grandparents in different parts of the world. It seemed pretty glamorous to a girl whose parents and grandparents and great-grandparents had all been from Melchester or the villages around it.

'What happens when it lands?' Rocky asked Helena quietly. She was embarrassed to be nervous, so kept her voice down even though she wanted to hear it from Helena and Priscilla ahead of experiencing it.

'You bounce a bit when you hit the runway,' Priscilla said, 'then the reverse engines come on and it's a bit noisy and you rock about a bit and you wonder if the plane is going to spin off the runway, but it's normal.'

'Normal? It doesn't sound normal.'

Anxious now, Rocky wished she was on a football pitch, her studs stuck firmly in the mud, knowing what was going on, free to do what she wanted, go where she wanted. She could cope with that. That's when she was at her happiest. Calm, in control, not in a tumult like this.

'Count to twenty as soon as you feel the wheels hit the runway,' Helena suggested, leaning over Priscilla, seeing Rocky's face going pale. 'When you get to twenty it's over, nothing bad can happen then. The plane will have slowed down and we'll be moving at the same speed as a car on a motorway.'

'And if I don't get to twenty?'

Helena shrugged. 'You're more likely to be killed in a car or a train or crossing the road than in a plane.'

'Is that true or is it just a made-up fact you can say to people who are scared of flying?'

Helena laughed. 'Dunno. I... maybe you're right.'

Rocky swallowed and nodded as the view of streets of houses, factories, motorways and car parks came closer and closer. So close she clenched everything, expecting impact.

*Bump.* There it was.

*Bump. Bump. Bump.*

'One, two, three…'

Rocky screwed her eyes tight and felt a rush of adrenaline as she counted and – as she did – she thought of her mum and how they were separated. That if she were to die now she'd be thousands of miles away from Melchester and Mum – and how that just didn't feel right.

It felt weird being in the air. It also felt weird she was away from Mum. Wrong, even. And there was a reason for that. A good one.

Rocky's dad was dead.

Mum needed her.

'Six, seven, eight…'

*What if she died too?*

*What would Mum do then?*

'Eleven, twelve…'

And – in that moment, the plane juddering down the runway – Rocky vowed she'd never do this again, never leave her mum. She would stay with her forever and make sure she was okay forever, because she felt quite sure now that it wasn't right to leave home, to leave Mum. Even though it was something she had always wanted to do.

'Eighteen, nineteen, twenty…'

The plane really did feel like it was under control now. It was going no faster than a coach on the motorway or a train. Just like Helena had said. Rocky turned to grin at her teammate.

'That was okay,' she admitted, then noticed Priscilla and Helena share a smile.

Rocky looked behind her and saw the rest of the Melchester Rovers players. The women's team and the men's, all peering out of the windows, checking out what Bulgaria looked like.

It was strange for Rocky. She had been so anxious about flying that she had forgotten who she was with, where they were going. So now she felt a rush of excitement. That she could afford to be excited now that they had landed. Excited that they were somewhere new, somewhere different. She felt she could get used to travel. If she got over the fear of flying.

Rocky Race and her teammates had arrived at the far side of Europe for a Europa Cup match against Spartak Lensburg. The men were here for that anyway. The women's team were here to get a taste for adventure. That's what their new Dutch coach, Serina Heracles, had said.

'We watch the men play in Europe. We

get a taste for European football, we get a taste for glory. Then, when we play at home, in England, we learn that, when we win and win again, we will one day play in Europe. Yes?'

Rocky loved her new coach. Melchester Rovers Women's team were gearing up to become a fully professional team next season. And that meant that they were on a path towards the elite game where – if they did well – they'd be in the top flight, within touching distance of Europe. Of trips like this where they would be the players.

And the funny thing about Serina Heracles was that she made Rocky feel like that would happen. Made her feel like – if she worked hard and took the right decisions – she would be an elite and professional footballer one day and could play anywhere she wanted in the world.

She had never felt like this before. And in that moment Rocky made another vow.

Rocky was determined to make that happen. She would follow this woman to the ends of the earth, take a thousand flights if she had to, so that another of her dreams could come true.

Her most-dreamed dream of them all: that, one day, she would become a professional footballer.

HAVING LANDED, COME through customs and navigated passport control, the Melchester men's and women's teams followed each other out into the arrivals hall. They passed giant banners saying 'Welcome to Lensburg' along the long glass corridors that channelled them towards a gallery full of glitzy shops and cafés. There was a reception committee in the large stark arrivals hall, where each of the players from both teams were gifted a box of chocolates wrapped in a traditional scarf.

'They're lovely, aren't they?' Helena said. 'The locals.'

Priscilla nodded. 'Really lovely,' she smiled.

Through two sliding doors, Rocky felt a blast of cold air and zipped up her red and yellow tracksuit top. They were outside. The sky was blue and bright. Rocky took a deep breath. She loved fresh air. Especially after hours and hours of recycled air in airports and aeroplanes. Breathing in, she realised she actually felt happy. Happy for the first time in a long while.

A LUXURY COACH was waiting for the Melchester party. Rocky watched as the men's team loaded their luggage into the bottom of the bus, her brother, Roy, chatting with Asif Mirza, the men's team winger.

Rocky liked most of Roy's teammates, but she especially had time for Asif. Even though he was a Championship player in the men's game, he always seemed too excited to be one. He never took it for granted, or was arrogant. Rocky knew people thought Roy was down to earth, but Asif was even more like that. He was like he'd always been, even when she'd known him as a sixteen-year-old lad in his debut season. Asif was kind, quiet and certainly not full of himself.

Like some of the men's squad.

Rocky was thinking of Jimmy Slade in particular.

Urgh.

The new Melchester Men's signing. Rocky couldn't bear him. And it was funny... the thing that really irritated her about Jimmy was that he was always having a go at Roy.

It had puzzled Rocky for a while. Why did it bother her that Jimmy Slade was always trying to wind up her brother? Because winding up Roy was something she had spent her life revelling in, laughing about, enjoying, and it was something she was particularly good at. So why was it a problem that Jimmy Slade was doing it too?

The answer was simple. Having a go at Roy was her job. And her job only. No one else got to do that.

Rocky stopped herself thinking about Jimmy Slade and tried to listen in to what her brother and Asif were saying to each other in the car park. She heard Asif say: 'I can't believe we are actually playing European football. I mean... here we are playing a team from abroad. They've played in the Champions League. They drew with Inter St Compostela three seasons ago.'

Rocky was about to shout across at Asif that he had earned his place at the top table of European football – or something like that – when she saw something that didn't look quite right.

A pair of white men standing on the other side of the road.

They were in front of a multi-storey car park with several of the country's national flags draped down the sides. The two men were standing, legs apart, hands on hips, staring hard at Asif and the rest of the squad.

*Weird*, Rocky thought. But why? Why did she feel weird?

She sensed the air cool around her.

Rocky realised that at the same time she had spotted the two men, Asif had seen them too, noticing no doubt how particularly aggressive they looked. It was something about their stance, their body language, the expressions on their faces that made it look like they hated Asif. It was so obvious. They'd singled him out with their menacing stares.

But why? Why would you hate Asif?

Rocky pointed the men out to Priscilla and Helena.

Priscilla studied them for a moment, then scrunched up her face.

'What?' Rocky asked.

Then Helena said, 'Come on,' and pulled at Rocky.

'Why?' Rocky asked. 'What's up?'

'Let's just get on the bus,' Priscilla added.

It was at times like this – along with when they were about to land – that Rocky remembered she was younger than some of her teammates, that half the time she didn't really know what was going on and had to defer to some of the others to explain things to her. They were older. She trusted them. She should do what they said and ask questions later. Rocky was comfortable with that, so she followed without any more fuss.

As they climbed aboard the luxury coach

and eased into their comfortable heated seats, Rocky definitely felt like she had missed something.

'Are their fans crazy or something?' she asked. 'I mean hooligans? Is that what's going on? You know? I mean, what that was about? Are they going to stand outside the team hotel and chant all night to keep the players awake? Stuff like that?'

Rocky had often thought it would be fun to do something like that at the hotel away teams stayed at in Melchester.

The engine started up and a warm flow of air rippled through the coach. Rocky had spotted more young men gathering now. Except some of them weren't that young, really. They were middle aged. Tired-looking. Beer-bellied. Some had baseball caps on. Others had hoods up. But the one thing they did have in common was that all of them looked scary. Rocky reckoned it was something to do with the way they were standing and the looks on their faces.

They looked mean. Really mean. And she was pretty sure they wanted to look like that.

Even so, Rocky felt an urge to walk over to them, stare them in the face and say: *What? What are you looking at?* It was like they were playground bullies who just needed someone to stand up to them. And Rocky had done some of that in her time.

'They call themselves Ultras,' Priscilla explained. 'Like hooligans in England, but they have an influence on the team too. They're sort of in with the players and even the owners of the club. It's hard to understand. They have a really bad reputation for violence and for being racist. Whenever they play teams with Black players or Asian players, anyone who's not white – they shout stuff and throw things, set off flares. And they get away with it.'

Rocky leaned back and smiled at Helena.

'Er... why are you smiling?' Priscilla asked.

'Because you're joking...' Rocky said. Then suddenly feeling chastened and young again compared to her teammates, she added, 'Aren't you? I mean... that's not real, is it? People aren't like that really.'

Helena leaned forward. 'She's not joking. It's true.'

'Oh... I'm sorry.' Rocky felt stupid. What was she going on about to Helena and Priscilla? She could hear herself now and how naïve she sounded. She wondered what her teammates must think of her.

Then a sudden thud.

A crack on the side of the coach.

Everyone ducked to watch a massive bin

bounce off the window, its contents splurging over the glass.

Rocky was on her feet now. Her instinctive reaction. She'd had enough of this. She'd go out there. Wanting to confront them, she shrugged off Priscilla's arms trying to keep her in her seat. And Helena telling her to leave it. In the aisle now, Rocky intended to head for the side door, but found herself staggering, as the coach driver fired the engine and the Melchester Rovers bus swiftly moved off.

Dumped back in her seat by the momentum of the bus, Rocky saw the group of men that Priscilla had called Ultras run in the other direction, pursued by a police van that was accelerating towards them from a side road. It all happened so quickly.

Welcome to Lensburg.

THE SPARTAK LENSBURG stadium was full over an hour before kick off. Huge open stands gave the fans views of a range of spectacular mountains in the background, a wide river winding its way through a city of spires and domes and lines of dark green trees.

Beautiful.

Rocky felt that buzz of excitement you feel when you go to watch your team play away. She'd seen what a glorious place they were in. And – apart from that small group of Ultras at the airport – the locals had been really warm and welcoming.

She felt more settled now. It had taken her a while to calm herself after the incident on the bus. She had felt so fired up and would 100% have gone to challenge the men. Or felt like it at the time. But she was kind of glad Priscilla and Helena had held her back.

Three hundred Melchester Rovers fans were a small patch of red and yellow amid a sea of blue and white. Rocky had calculated that the Melchester fans were outnumbered a hundred to one.

In the minority.

And any singing from the Melchester end was drowned out by the raucous roaring of the home fans. But Rocky still felt amazing. Excited. Proud of who they were. This was so different to what she was used to, so new.

Rocky was discovering that when you travel sometimes you feel like the world is opening up around you all new and exciting, but that sometimes you wish you were back home in your bedroom with the door closed and your favourite playlist on.

It was a shock for Rocky to realise that this was the first time since Dad had died that she had felt excited.

Because she was, wasn't she?

Excited?

And that was good, wasn't it?

She needed to feel excited again. She needed to grieve, but she needed to live too. Be a person who felt normal feelings again. Dad would have wanted that more than anything.

*Dad would have loved this*, she thought with a grin.

And – her mind back on the football – Rocky was thinking what if they could win here? And thinking of Dad again… Wouldn't it be good if he was here to see this? But then she frowned. She was always thinking that about everything.

If only Dad was here…

Dad would have loved this…

It's such a shame that Dad Dad Dad…

Rocky sighed and tried to drag her thoughts away from the sadness about Dad and back to the football.

This could be exciting. She wanted to live it. Rocky reminded herself what was going on. A second-tier men's team from England was playing against a football club that was the best in its country. And it was her team that was doing it. Melchester Rovers.

Did these things actually happen in real life? It was like something out of a children's story book. But Rocky could feel her feet planted on the concrete beneath her. She stamped them, grinning. It was real. She was here.

As she watched the Rovers Men's players warm up, she felt proud. What if Roy and Asif and the others could do it? What if they could come over a thousand miles from home and win?

Rocky glanced at her manager – Serina Heracles – to see her coach looking back at her, as if she was trying to read Rocky's mind.

'One day, this is you,' Heracles told her. 'This can be your future.'

Rocky grinned. It was exciting enough watching the men's team she had supported all her life playing in a far-off city on the other side of Europe. But to be told this could be her future? That she could be playing for the best English women's teams away in Europe? That that could be her life?

*Beyond dreams*, she thought.

Then, no. Not beyond dreams. It was

a dream. She could do it. She could be a professional footballer playing in the top flight, in Europe, like her brother. Maybe one day for her country. She wanted to wear an England top. If he could do things like that, why not her?

There was hope. There was a chance to be happy.

Yes, things had been tough. Yes, she had lost her dad. But there were still things worth living for. There was football.

SPARTAK LENSBURG VERSUS Melchester Rovers started at a frantic pace and – for the first few minutes – Melchester Rovers Men looked to be in shock. Overwhelmed.

It wasn't just the intense pressing of the Spartak team. It was the crowd too. Every time Melchester got the ball, they'd whistle.

Like in England when a crowd wants the ref to finish the game, but this whistling went on all the time. Then there was shouting and flares going off in the stands, great fireworks of red and orange, burning, seeming to suck all the light out of the rest of the stadium. Fans jumping up and down, twirling scarves above their heads. Such a strange atmosphere. Rocky imagined it must be hard to play with all those distractions going on. It wasn't that it was intimidating: it was just so different from an English football crowd.

But after a little while the passion of the home fans waned. The atmosphere softened. And Rocky could sense a change on the pitch as a result. The intensity was ebbing away from the team playing in blue and white.

'That's all they've got,' Helena said to Rocky, laughing.

'They threw everything into the first

fifteen minutes,' Priscilla added. 'Now it's our turn.'

And so it was.

With twenty minutes on the clock Melchester Rovers Men began to assert themselves onto the game. Will Gray broke into the area, sudden and aggressive, and hammered a shot just over the bar. More whistling from the home fans.

Rocky looked at Priscilla. She had been right: now it was Melchester's turn. Rocky loved how Priscilla and Helena could read the game. Now that the women's team had new investment, new hopes and, most importantly, new players, signed from all over the country, even one from the US, Rocky was aware that she was surrounded by football expertise that she could learn from.

Experience.

Maturity.

And that she had new friends like Priscilla and Helena that she could talk football with.

'They're backing off,' Rocky said.

'Inviting us onto them. Exactly,' Helena said.

Another Mel Rovers attack. Asif Mirza ran down the wing, boos ringing out above the sound of the whistles as he laid it back to Vernon Elliott, who dinked a ball into Roy, back to goal.

Rocky knew what was coming and watched as Roy half-turned in a second and slammed a shot in towards the inside of the right-hand post.

It was a good strike. Powerful. But the Spartak keeper got down to palm it away for a corner.

More shouting above the whistles.

Another flare going off.

'It's so hostile,' Priscilla shouted above the noise.

Helena nodded, scanning the home fans, then pointing at a particular group of fans. 'That lot. I don't like that lot. Listen.'

Rocky tried to listen. There was some sort of chanting masked by the sound of the whistling and the shouting. A low noise. And she felt the skin on her arms prickle. It was hard to know why or what the issue was, but she felt weird, uneasy.

Positive feelings began to drain away as Rocky saw Asif looking into the home fans. And that was weird too. Very weird. Asif was always 100% mind-on-the-pitch. But he seemed distracted somehow. Really not like him at all.

Rocky watched Roy jog up to Asif and look into his eyes, close up, holding him by both shoulders as if he was trying to get him to focus. Talking to him, face to face.

*Strange game*, Rocky thought, as play began again. *We're so out of character. Is it the whistling?*

Then, her eye off the match for a second too long, Rocky realised that the game had moved on and Roy was in again. Another shot on goal. From six yards. But somehow the Spartak keeper was down again, heroic, fending the shot away. *He was a hell of a keeper*, Rocky thought to herself.

'Go on, Vernon! Hit it!' Rocky heard herself shout, watching the ball ricochet back at the players. Vernon Elliott was there. Following up. Cracking the ball hard and into the roof of the net as Rocky launched herself into the air and roared, her throat hurting.

'Yessssssss!'

They'd scored. Rocky's team were winning.

For a few seconds the sound of Melchester Rovers' three hundred travelling fans echoed around a stunned Spartak stadium as Vernon Elliott stood, arms in the air towards the away end, Roy and Will Gray grabbing him from behind to celebrate, all three of them looking up into the stand where their fans were celebrating.

Then Rocky saw a blur of yellow. Something from the stands. It flickered, catching the floodlights' glare. And then Roy was down. Squatting. Hand to his head.

Rocky made a noise like a scream or a shout.

Had the thing hit him?

What was it?

A flare?

Her brother. Hit by a missile, something.

What had they done?

'Roooooooooooyyyyy!!!!' she bellowed.

Rocky felt like her intestines were being ripped out. No one hurt her brother. He was everything to her. She heard herself call out his name again.

And then, not thinking, she was trying to get down to him, climb through the fans. But it was impossible to get past so many people standing and raging.

Rocky heard Priscilla shouting now. 'Lofty's down!'

'It was a coin!' Helena was screaming. 'He's been hit by a coin.'

So much going on. Too much. It was hard to think. Impossible. And amid the screaming and booing, Rocky, trying to make sense of what was going on in front of her eyes, could hear the strange noises again. A weird chanting. But she could see that Roy was on his feet now, though Lofty Peak was still down. She gasped in some of the cool evening air.

Then she heard something. Saw Priscilla pressing the sides of her head with rage.

'What is that?' Rocky asked. 'Are you okay?'

'Monkey noises,' Priscilla groaned. 'They're making monkey noises. And that thing that hit your brother. It was a banana.'

Even if she couldn't believe it, Rocky understood what Priscilla had said to her. She had heard about this, but she never thought it could happen. Not really happen.

Racist fans throwing bananas at Black players.

Racist fans making monkey noises.

Now even more noise around them, more chaos in front of them.

Rocky stared at Priscilla, then Helena,

but neither would catch her eye. They were looking hard at the pitch. So Rocky did so too, struggling to see what was happening there. The Melchester Rovers players had gathered in a huddle in the centre of pitch, out of the range of the supporters' missiles.

Vernon and Asif and Roy and Will with all the others were grouped tight, all their yellow and red shirts as one, whereas the blue and white of the Spartak team was dotted around the pitch, their players staring into the stands in ones and twos. Everything was so strange, dislocated, disparate.

And now – on top of everything – Rocky could smell burning.


THE MELCHESTER MEN, she could see, were talking. The referee seemed to be watching them. Calling over with questions now.

Looking like he was annoyed with the Melchester players, not everyone else.

Rocky didn't get that. Why wasn't the referee doing something? And where were the stewards or the police? Why weren't they doing anything? Why was this happening?

Rocky saw one of the Melchester stewards run across the pitch from the Melchester fans to the players, to Roy. The Rovers always brought their own stewards with them to away games. It helped avoid trouble if their fans were being controlled by familiar faces. That was common practice.

Rocky watched the players and the steward and now the Melchester bench talking. What the hell were they talking about?

And then – after a few moments of confused gesturing and nodding and conversation – they walked.

It was hard to believe it was happening.

But it was happening.

The whole Melchester Rovers team was walking.

Off the pitch.

To the sound of goading and more whistling from the Spartak fans.

Rocky looked at her friends to see that Priscilla had her mouth wide open.

'I don't get it,' Rocky shouted. She had been at dozens of football games and it looked to her as if Melchester Men were heading to the dressing rooms at half time or something. But it wasn't half time.

Helena said what they had all realised was happening. 'They're coming off.'

'What?' Rocky asked above the roars and screams of derision coming from the home fans. She felt such a deep urge to get at the home fans now, to just run at them and shut them up.

'They're refusing to play,' Priscilla explained. 'Because of the abuse our players are getting.' She had tears coming down her cheeks. But she was smiling too. Grinning.

'Good,' Helena said.

'No one has ever done this before,' Priscilla said.

'We'll be booted out of the tournament,' Rocky heard someone else shouting. Someone behind them. 'Look at the ref. He's telling Roy: leave the pitch and we're out of the tournament.'

'So what?' Rocky said, turning round to answer him. 'Who wants to play against scum like this?'

'Let's turn our backs,' Priscilla said. 'We need to show what we think of the Spartak fans. Come on.'

Rocky nodded. It was a good idea. Show their disgust too. Like the players. And

Rocky knew that – although she had the instinct to run up to the home fans and start on them – this was better. She would follow Priscilla's lead.

So, as Melchester Men walked off the pitch and out of the tournament, the noise and rage and booing getting louder and louder, Rocky joined Priscilla and Helena turning their backs. And now she could see that all the Melchester fans were doing the same. The backs of their heads only visible to the rest of the stadium. Facing the back of the stand, staring at the mountain range behind them, the clouds gathering above them and then – at just that moment – blocking the setting sun.

It was as if nature was as appalled as Rocky and Priscilla and Helena were. By what it had seen. By what it had heard. And was now showing how it felt.

AFTER THE GAME – when all the fans had left the stadium and the match had been awarded as a 3–0 victory to Spartak – the unused men's substitutes and the women's team were allowed onto the pitch for a training session.

A very apologetic Spartak club official stood with them.

'It is safe here now. There is only you here. No fans. And please... Anything you need,' she said, to a background noise of chanting and sirens and the flash of flares coming from outside the stadium, 'please ask me. I am ashamed of my club. I am so sorry.'

Serina Heracles formed a large circle with the twenty or so players who had come out for the training session. They concentrated on one-touch passing at speed. Rocky knew why she had done this: she was making sure everyone was together, focusing on each other, not the noises she could still hear from outside the stadium and the memories of what had just happened here.

Football. Only football.

The team. Each other. Together stronger.

Now that night was falling a dew was forming on the pitch, causing the ball to zip off the grass quickly, meaning it was hard to control. Rocky knew how much the first touch of the ball meant to their new coach and she gave it everything to make sure that the first touch was perfect, that she controlled the ball, then was able to pass it, at pace, to the player opposite her.

Even though she understood exactly what her coach wanted to achieve, Rocky longed to see Roy and check out how he was feeling, but the men's team who had just played and come off were still in the dressing rooms. She would have to wait. Wait and concentrate. *Football. Only football.* This was something that worked for Rocky. If she was troubled or distracted – even unhappy – she could use focusing on football alone to bring calm to her mind, to try to be a tiny bit happier. And by focusing on the ball, not her thoughts, she managed to control and pass the ball perfectly every time. While some other players needed two touches or tried to be a bit too flash, Rocky gave 100% to the basics.

After the passing, the players were asked to run a few laps of the pitch, nice and gentle, to warm down before they travelled back to the airport. Caught up in the training now,

Rocky sensed someone running alongside her and looked up, hoping it was Roy.

It was Serina Heracles.

'Boss?' she said.

'You are okay, Rocky?'

'Thanks, yes.'

They jogged a few paces side by side.

'You have good focus.'

'Thanks, boss.'

'I see you. I imagine you worry about your brother. I see, though, you still can play perfect precise football. And this tells me clearly that when we need you, when we are under the most pressure in a game, I can rely on you. You understand me? I can see what you are capable of. Great things. I will need you.'

Rocky nodded and felt a shudder of excitement. She breathed in. She didn't want to betray how emotional she was feeling that her coach was so positive about her part in the team. She wanted to keep it all in. For now.

'Thanks, boss,' she said again.

Then, reaching the far end of the pitch together – where the incidents had happened earlier in the game – Rocky saw a banana on the pitch. She stooped to pick it up and held it in front of her.

'How do you feel about that?' Heracles asked, studying Rocky's face.

Rocky didn't know how to answer. She always wanted to give the best reply to her coach. To impress her. But this was harder.

*How do I feel that some of my brother's teammates and my friends – Vernon and Asif and Lofty – had bananas thrown at them, monkey noises shouted at them? Because of the colour of their skin?*

The sky was dark now. The floodlights

were still on and all Rocky could see was a ghost of the mountains behind the city. Rocky looked at the banana.

'I don't know,' she said. 'Upset? Angry? Ashamed? I'm feeling a few things and I don't think there's one word for them.'

Serina Heracles nodded. 'Good answers to a difficult question. Maybe I should ask

a better question. What does it make you want to do?'

'Help make it stop,' Rocky said without thinking.

'A quick answer. And a good answer. How do you help make this stop?'

Rocky felt a sense of panic. Questions like this were hard. She was worried she would say the wrong thing. But questions like this needed answering too. She knew that. She would say what came into her mind and if someone thought it was wrong, they could tell her and she might change her mind. Better that than say what you thought people wanted to hear. Better to be honest. She wasn't scared of being corrected or of learning.

Also she wanted to find out how her coach felt. How did all of that make her feel?

'By standing up to it, standing with those

it's happening to,' Rocky said. 'Calling it out.'

Serina Heracles nodded. 'That's good. Will you do that?'

Rocky nodded. 'I will.'

Then – as they turned again – Rocky saw her brother on the far side of the stadium, emerging from the tunnel, flanked by Vernon Elliott and Lofty Peak who had a bandage on his head. She couldn't help but stare over at him.

'Can I go over?' she asked. 'I'm sorry. I want to see my friends, my brother.'

'Yes. Go.'

Tossing the banana to the sidelines, Rocky ran across the pitch and – smiling at her brother first – gave Lofty, then Vernon, a hug.

'Are you okay?' she said, stepping back and looking at them, as her brother stood at her side.

'Yeah. Thanks, Rocky,' they both replied.

Rocky knew they weren't. Both Vernon and Lofty looked tired. Really tired.

Now more of the women's team came over to chat with the men, giving Rocky a chance to speak to Roy. She looked at his forehead, where the banana had hit him, then reached out and touched it. There was a red mark, but the skin hadn't been broken.

'So how are you, then?' she asked.

Roy shrugged and made a face she knew well from all the years they had been together as children. A crumpled face with a pretend smile. The kind of face she'd seen and would turn to call Mum or Dad to come and help. But, here they were, adults pretty much, hundreds of miles from home and having to deal with stuff themselves.

'You did the right thing,' she said. 'Coming off the pitch. No one ever does that. But you did and I am proud of you all.'

'Thanks,' Roy said, staring into the intense light of the floodlights, his irises like pinheads. 'Lofty and Vernon had the idea. I thought it was the right thing to do too. We all did. It was a team decision.'

'A good one,' Rocky said.

'We're out of Europe,' he added.

'I know.'

'I might never play in Europe again,' he said.

'You might not,' Rocky said.

They shared a long comfortable silence.

'Did you see us all turning our backs?' Rocky asked.

Roy's eyes lit up for a second. 'Yeah. That was good.'

'Priscilla's idea,' Rocky said.

'Great idea...' Roy's voice tailed off.

Another silence. Rocky felt like she should say something. Her brother had done something good, but he felt bad. He needed her to be positive.

'But, if you do play in Europe again,' Rocky told him, 'and I am pretty sure you will, you might not have to face that kind of rubbish again. Because of what Lofty and Vernon and Asif and you and all the others just did.'

'You reckon?'

Rocky remembered what Serina Heracles had said to her. *How do you make it stop? By standing up to it, calling it out.*

'I do,' she said. 'And, if you never play in Europe again, you and the others can all be proud that you did what you did. That's better than a goal or a trophy or anything. I've been your little sister for seventeen years and I've seen you do all sorts of amazing things. And – even though I take the mick and all that – I have always been proud of you. But what you and the others just did out there? That's the thing that's made me feel the most proud.'

Now Rocky saw Asif standing alone, staring into the empty stands.

'I'm off to see if Asif is okay,' Rocky told her brother. 'Are you all right?'

'I'll survive,' Roy nodded. 'And thanks.'

'For what?'

'For what you just said. It was nice.'

Rocky smiled and gave her brother a friendly kick on the back of his leg and went to speak to Asif.

A BLAST OF noise and light hit Rocky as the automatic doors opened.

They were home. Back at Melchester Airport.

It was the next day and it was hard to think that the bleak events of the night before had really happened.

Until arrivals. Until now.

One minute they were walking calmly along clean empty corridors, with only the sound of their footsteps and very little conversation among the Melchester men's or women's teams, then the doors opened and they were back in the real world.

Flashes of cameras. Questions shouted. Noise and light bouncing off the huge sheets of glass that formed the front of the arrivals hall.

Rocky had positioned herself alongside her brother and Lofty and Vernon and Asif. She had been expecting something like this. And she wanted to walk with them.

The first question was flung at them by the media. 'How do you feel now you've been booted out of Europe?'

Then: 'Do you regret coming off the pitch now? Now you're out of the tournament? Do you think you let Melchester down?'

There were chants from fans, background noise to the questions being fired at the team.

*Rovers! Rovers! Rovers!*

*One Vernon Elliott. There's only one Vernon Elliott.*

*We love you, Mirza, we do...*

Good supportive stuff coming from dozens of men and women and children in club shirts and scarves.

'It doesn't sound like the fans think that!' Rocky shouted in response to the stupid journalists' questions, but nobody heard her above the clamour.

And then she heard booing.

Just as Rocky came to a stop and watched someone from the club begin to usher the players through the double doors that had opened suddenly at the edge of arrivals.

She heard one of her teammates calling to her.

'Rocky? Rocky? This way...'

*But booing?*

Rocky's attention was on the fans, not her teammates. Someone was booing? Who were they booing? And why? Was that actually happening? It took a lot for Rocky to keep control, not to react.

Then – with a break in the boos – a shout.

'Where are you running off to, cowards?'

Followed by a chant from a small group of fans.

*What the heck…*
*What the heck…*
*What the heck is going on?*

And – amid the melee – Rocky sensed that familiar click in her head. The click that came when she felt the need to do something or say something, even though she knew it could backfire. Kind of like at the Spartak stadium the night before, when she wanted to run onto the pitch but had been held back. Or on the coach before that when the so-called Ultras were being so vile. Some people called it red mist. Others called it losing her head. And it was something that mostly happened to her on the pitch. Not off it.

Off it, she usually kept some sort of control.

But not today. Not this time. No one was going to have a go at her friends. No one was going to call them that.

Cowards?

Really?

Forgetting Roy, Asif and the others, Rocky strode towards the small group of fans. The wide grins on their faces faded as she stood in front of them and one of the TV cameras was turned to focus on them, the light coming from beneath its lens bright in their and Rocky's eyes.

'What are you doing?' Rocky asked. She'd give them a chance, try to talk nicely.

The one woman among the small group of fans stepped forward, narrowing her eyes to look at Rocky. The men with her all seemed to step back at the same time. There was a metal barrier between Rocky and the woman. The woman was using it to lean forward.

'Protesting,' she said.

'Protesting?' Rocky couldn't prevent

herself laughing. 'What are you protesting about? Global warming? Against the government's treatment of refugees? What's your big issue?'

The woman smiled back, then leaned closer. 'You think you're clever, don't you? But I know who you are,' she said, staring hard at Rocky.

Rocky nodded. What was that? A threat?

Deep down she knew she should back off and avoid confrontation. Step away from conflict. Think about it. Don't do anything rash. It is what her mum had always said they should do, but Rocky could never do that.

'Well, you're one up on me, then,' Rocky said.

There was a short silence, then the men with the woman laughed at Rocky's joke, causing the woman to scowl at Rocky, maintaining her fierce eye-contact, leaning even further forward on the metal barrier, glowering. But saying nothing.

'You've still not explained to me what you're protesting about,' Rocky said.

'Your brother and his teammates wimping out last night,' the woman said. 'That's what.'

'Wimping out?'

'Yes. And being cowards.'

'Cowards? Are you serious?'

'I'm deadly serious.'

There was a small crowd round Rocky and her rival now. And she realised this was important. She also noticed that she was alone. All the other players – from the women's and men's teams – had disappeared through the double doors, which were now shut.

She'd have to catch a bus home, she thought. *Oh well*. She could cope with that.

And – anyway – that didn't matter yet. What mattered was winning the argument with this horrible woman. Rocky studied her. She was wearing a Melchester Rovers top. An old one. Rocky remembered Dad used to have that one when she was a kid. But she didn't let that put her off. She knew how Dad would feel about the players coming off the pitch. He would have backed them 100%. Rocky felt like her dad was there, with her, on her shoulder.

'What sort of a football shirt do you want to wear?' Rocky asked, glancing down at the woman's Melchester Rovers shirt.

'This one,' the woman sneered, pulling the badge to her lips and kissing it.

'Me too,' Rocky said. 'And what sort of team do you want to support?'

'This one. Are you stupid? Can't you see what shirt I've got on?' The woman sounded exasperated. Like she thought Rocky was an idiot.

*She doesn't understand*, Rocky thought.

'But what sort of team?' Rocky tried again. 'One that people will remember as a team that stands up against what's wrong? Or one that just lets bad stuff happen and pretends it doesn't matter?'

'Bad stuff? Like being kicked out of Europe? That's what's bad.'

Rocky shook her head. 'The bad stuff is the racist abuse that was aimed at our players. Were you there? I mean, at the game? Did you travel?'

'I watched it on TV,' the woman replied, all of a sudden slightly defensive.

'Well, I was there,' Rocky said, feeling like she should give the woman a chance, not just attack her, create conflict. 'Look. I saw it. I heard it. It was horrible. The players did the right thing. If you had been there, you'd know what I mean. I promise you.'

'I doubt it,' the woman replied.

Rocky felt her head begin to ache and fizzle. That red mist was coming. But she wanted to talk about it, do what Serina Heracles had told her to do. Call it out.

'How would you feel if someone made monkey noises at you?'

The woman laughed. 'Well, they wouldn't, would they?'

Rocky felt her throat tightening. And she knew she was losing control of what she wanted to say. She felt like her head was in flames as she heard herself speaking.

'What if they had a go at you for being scum? For being like a Neanderthal? Like some half-human piece of...'

Now the woman spat. At Rocky. Missing her target.

There was a reaction from the crowd around her. Shock. Disgust. Even the men who were standing with her looked disgusted.

Rocky stepped back, then lunged at the woman, but found herself being taken by the back of her coat. Pulled back. She looked to her side. What was this? Was she being arrested? Or dragged into another argument?

It was Mum.

'Come on. I've got the car,' Mum said.

Rocky breathed out and let herself be pulled by her mum away from the cameras and the horrible woman, still ranting. They were out of the melee now, through the giant airport doors, into the crisp fresh air. She took a deep breath of autumn and smiled as she heard the voice of her rival fade then be silenced by the sliding doors easing shut. She was in shock. She thought she had left unpleasant people behind in the country they'd just flown out of, but now she understood there were unpleasant people with offensive views everywhere, in England, even in her beloved Melchester.

'Who was your friend?' Mum asked.

'I didn't…' Rocky heard herself say.

'Did she hit you?'

'No. But she… I…'

'Let's get you home.' Mum's voice was calm and quiet and comforting. Now Rocky heard herself let out a sound like a sob, Mum's grip on her arm suddenly firmer. Rocky coughed to mask her sob and let herself be led.

The car was in the short stay car park opposite the entrance. They walked up several flights of a stone staircase and through a heavy door. Lights flickered on as they walked past dozens of cars. There was a pervading smell of exhaust fumes and wee. Rocky could definitely smell wee. She coughed again, wondered if she was going to be sick. She was glad to get into the car and smell the familiar scent of the air freshener Mum kept in the car. It smelled like vanilla. It smelled like safety. Like Mum.

'Thanks, Mum,' Rocky whispered.

Then they were driving. In silence as they went down four floors of the multi-storey car park, round and round, then out to the barrier and flashing lights and traffic cones everywhere.

As they negotiated the airport parking exits, Rocky sensed Mum studying her. She realised she, herself, was staring hard through the windscreen and – after a while – turned to look at Mum.

'You okay?' Mum asked.

'Yeah. Thanks. And thanks for coming for me. How did you know I'd miss the team bus?'

'Mother's intuition,' Mum smiled.

They drove on through a tunnel under the main runway, towards the city. Lights flickering. Bright, dark. Bright-dark. Rocky felt a headache coming on and pressed the sides of her skull, her mind a maelstrom of thoughts and feelings and memories that had been packed into the last few hours.

She scanned through texts from Roy, Priscilla and Helena.

**Where are you? Are you okay?**

Rocky replied quickly.

**Yes. Fine. Thanks. With Mum.**

Then her mind was back on the night before.

Foremost were the images of bananas

being thrown at the Black players in the Melchester Rovers team, the players walking off, then the look on the faces of Lofty and Vernon when she went to hug them after it had happened.

As if reading her mind, Mum asked 'How were the lads? Vernon? Asif? Lofty?'

Rocky didn't know what to say.

How were they?

How did Vernon feel?

Lofty? Asif?

She couldn't imagine. How did it feel to have something thrown at you and noises made at you because of what colour your skin was?

'I don't know,' Rocky told her mum.

5

MELCHESTER ROVERS WOMEN no longer trained at the local sports centre. Not since they had been invited to have equal access with the men's team to the state-of-the-art facilities at the Mel Park training complex. This meant that they no longer had to tolerate crumbling pitches and groups of men tapping their watches suggesting it was their turn to use the council facilities ten minutes before it actually was, thinking men had priority over women playing football because the game belonged to them.

It didn't.

One of the things Serina Heracles insisted on when she was offered the job as Head Coach was full access to all the club's training facilities. Parity for the women's and men's teams.

*Parity.* That was one of the words she used. Rocky didn't think it was a word she'd ever said out loud. But here was her coach using it every day. And not even in her own language. Serina Heracles was Dutch.

And what did parity mean?

A gym. Superb grass and 4G pitches. Indoor pitches too for when the weather was grim. In addition they had medical and physio support, led by Frankie Pepper, who had been at the club since the men's team rose from the Second Division.

It all made sense to Rocky now. Before they had parity, she had always wondered why – when you were playing FIFA – you had the option to spend money on upgrading your team's training facilities instead of buying players. What difference did it make having a gym or all weather pitches? How much effect was there from having a team of physiotherapists, a dietician? Did it make your players better? Really?

Rocky knew now that the answer was yes. 100% yes.

Even more so since Rocky heard regularly from her friend and former teammate, Ffion Guthrie, who was now in America playing for a university side with facilities that women footballers had only been able to dream of for decades.

When Ffion called Rocky and talked about football in the US, Rocky realised that all this she now had at Melchester Rovers would make a difference to her too. She just wished Ffion was here to share it with her.

Rocky missed her. A lot. But sometimes your best friend moved to live on the other side of the world and you just had to deal with it.

Get her head round Ffion being away.

Get her head round the idea that someone she knew could get a scholarship at an American university to be a footballer. *I mean… what a dream*. That was another dream Rocky sometimes dwelt on. What would that be like?

Her mind back on training, Rocky took in the grounds. She loved the indoor pitches. All week it had been icy and cold outside and had been raining for at least forty-eight hours. And the floodlights' glare gave her headaches. But inside. In here. In the indoor training facility. It was amazing.

Because it was warm and light and consistent, Rocky could really get stuck in and dominate the ball.

After warm up and drills, Melchester Rovers Women had a short seven-a-side match to finish up the training session.

This is what Rocky lived for. Football. Playing the game. She liked doing warm ups and drills because she knew they made a difference. They made her stronger, more flexible, they helped her develop new skills and fine-tune the skills she already had. And – for up to an hour – she could cope with that. Focusing on improving her game physically and mentally. But, really, what she lived for was the ball. She wanted to fight for possession of a football.

And today was especially good for that as she was playing in the middle against the club's other two midfielders, Eve Ainsworth and Narinder Mehmi. Two players who helped Rocky boss the midfield every time they played a full match.

Teammates. Friends. Players she respected more than most. But they were not teammates or friends during a training game. They were players she wanted to get the ball off, keep the ball off. Players she needed to shut down and keep out of the action.

Halfway into the match, a niggly 0–0 devoid of creativity and beautiful football and the kind of game that Rocky loved, she noticed Eve Ainsworth hesitate on the ball. Just for a moment.

It was something about the bounce. And the fact that Eve needed a second touch.

Rocky didn't wait for an invitation. She pounced, leading with her left foot, dragging the ball back, falling, then hands on the pitch to twist herself and get back onto her feet, she played a ball into Priscilla who had moved into space ahead of her. But in space alone.

Firmly back on her feet Rocky moved wide towards goal, feeling Narinder's knee in the back of her leg, but shrugging off the tackle and the insult muttered at her, as she received the ball left-footed from Priscilla while falling and half-volleyed it under Lily Halifax, the keeper.

There was a sudden and huge cheer. From both sides. Then laughter.

Rocky rolled her eyes, then looked back to see Serina Heracles clapping. What was this? Why was her coach clapping a goal in a seven-a-side training game?

'Is that the first time she's seen you score?' Narinder asked, putting her hand out to lift Rocky off the pitch.

Rocky nodded.

'Maybe she'll make you striker?' Eve smiled, rubbing her hands.

Rocky shuddered. 'No thanks.'

The training match went on and now Rocky made sure she played deeper. Far from the goal. She knew that Serina Heracles had a reputation for trying players out of position to help them develop. There was no way she was going to put herself forward as a potential goal scorer. She really didn't want that. She wanted to battle, break up creative play, she wanted to be a wrecking ball of a footballer.

Priscilla caught up with Rocky once the game was over.

'So some woman spat at you?' Priscilla asked.

'Yeah. But she missed.'

Priscilla smiled. 'What happened?'

'She didn't get why the men came off. We started arguing. She said something. Then I did. Then she spat at me and I tried to hit her, or maybe it was the other way round. I dunno. Then Mum dragged me back.'

Priscilla nodded. 'Did she get why they came off, why you disagreed with her?'

Rocky frowned. 'Maybe. I hope so. But possibly not. I lost it a bit.'

'I'm sorry we abandoned you,' Priscilla said.

'Yeah, but you didn't really, though. It was me going off on one.'

As Rocky and Priscilla came off the pitch, ready to jog home, Rocky was surprised to see someone waiting for her. Waving.

Seeing Roy appear pitch side, everything came back. All of it.

Her life. The things that existed off the football pitch.

It was so strange that when she was playing football now, nothing else came into her mind, nothing else mattered. The fact that she had a brother who was a Championship footballer in the men's game. That they lived with their mum in a small terraced house less than a mile from Mel Park. That their mum was a widow because – not so long ago – their dad had died after a long illness. All of that. All of the worry that came with that. About Mum.

They didn't have to worry so much about money, but they did have to worry about Mum and how she was doing now that she'd lost her soul mate and her children were adults, or almost adults.

Then there was the racist incident in Eastern Europe and how some fans and media were making out Roy and his teammates had done the wrong thing coming off the pitch. How they were blaming him for the club being booted out of Europe. How that made her mad. It was so unfair.

The real world. Rocky smiled to herself. She preferred the football world.

So why was her brother here?

'What's up?' she asked Roy.

'Gonna give you a lift,' Roy said. 'There's press everywhere.'

Rocky looked outside to see camera women and men and journalists chatting outside the training complex. But not the usual ones they normally spoke to after games. Local journos like Becky Goff were fine. She was there for the long run: she needed a relationship with Melchester Rovers so she had to be respectful. And she was.

But the new ones. The ones who only came when there was trouble, controversy, pain. She could see why they were called vultures. They only turned up when there was blood on the ground, when there was a chance there'd be more bloodshed too. The ones who would disappear and move on to the next football scandal, the next unpleasant source of controversy and anger that it could whip up in its readers and viewers. They were here. Still here.

'Urgh,' Rocky said.

'They'll ask you stuff. They'll follow you home. I've got Mum's car. Come with me.'

Rocky hated to be offered help. Especially by Roy. And a part of her wanted to have a go at the vultures, tell them what she thought of them. But she was tired. Tired and a bit sick of always wanting to wade into a fight. So this time she'd take the help. Get away.

Roy pulled out of the car park with at least two media cars on their tail. Everyone wanted a piece of the English football team captain who had taken his team off the pitch, causing them to be booted out of Europe. Roy took it steady, watching his pursuers in his rear-view mirror. Occasionally sighing.

'What do they even expect to get from you?' Rocky asked Roy.

'Photos of me looking angry. Me outside the house looking like I've got something in my eye. Me driving badly. Maybe us arguing. I don't know. Some image they can put on a newspaper or a webpage that they can add a few words to make me out to be stupid or corrupt or... I don't know...'

They approached a set of traffic lights at a crossroads on the inner ring road. Rocky sensed Roy slow down, then, just as the lights began to change, felt him accelerate, leaving the media cars stuck at a red light. He had timed it perfectly and had done nothing illegal or dangerous.

'Nice move,' Rocky laughed, as Roy took a gentle right up a tight country lane that headed steep up to the Moor.

'Interesting route?' Rocky muttered.

She had been thinking about what Priscilla had said. Whether that woman who spat at her had understood where Rocky was coming from, why Rocky agreed with the men coming off the pitch at Spartak. What had Priscilla meant asking that? That Rocky should have argued with the woman more? Or just walked away and left her to her nastiness?

'I reckon we sit on the Moor for half an hour,' Roy said, breaking into Rocky's thoughts. 'They'll only go to our house next. We need to make out we've gone out for a meal or something.'

It was dark now, away from the blanket street lighting and reflective signs that dominated the ring road. Roy had slowed down to make sure he was being safe.

'That's fine, bro,' Rocky said. She didn't mind not getting home straight away. Home was painful. There was no getting away from it. There was a dark cloud over their house and shadows in every room. That's how Rocky saw it. Grief, that was. Grief was dark, shadowy. It didn't help that it was autumn moving into winter now. Less light. Less warmth.

They parked up and Rocky asked her brother if they could get out of the car. She needed to stretch her legs after training. It was – she knew – not a good idea to do a full workout, then sit with your legs cramped in a car. You were asking for an injury doing that. A muscle strain that might take weeks to get rid of if you were unlucky.

'Why do you always come to the Moor?' Rocky asked her brother.

They were sitting on the edge of the Moor now, the city below, illuminated. A wind rushing up the hillside, ruffling their hair and causing the trees to swirl, the last leaves cascading around them.

'I feel good here,' Roy said.

Rocky wondered about asking him if he hated being at home and liked it here because it didn't remind him of Dad being gone and Mum being lonely and the darkness and shadow that preyed on her mind, but she didn't. She was scared of the answer. Scared what it would mean for Mum. For all of them. Imagine them both agreeing that Mum made them feel sad or even annoyed them. How heartbreakingly disloyal would that be?

Rocky studied her brother's face. He looked calm. Almost happy. Whereas she felt like her stomach was being twisted round and round, tighter and tighter. She hated being inside her own head sometimes.

'You feel good?' she asked Roy, trying

to distract herself. 'Really. Sitting here, Melchester below us. You feel good?'

Roy nodded. 'Course.'

Rocky couldn't understand it. What was there to feel good about? Away from the football – for her – she was struggling to avoid feeling bad all the time. And it came to her – in a lightbulb moment – that something had to change. But what? What could you change?

'Why?' Roy asked, studying her. 'Don't you?'

'Why don't I what?' Rocky had lost the thread of their conversation.

'Don't you feel good sitting here?' her brother said.

Rocky paused. All the thoughts she'd had for weeks since Dad died. Half-thoughts even. Things she didn't dare say or even think about. And here was a chance to try to articulate what she was feeling, how she really was.

This restlessness.

'No,' she said.

And then they both saw a movement on the edge of the trees fifty metres to their left. A deer. A deer with antlers, sniffing the air.

They gazed, grinning at the deer.

'Why?' Roy whispered. 'Aren't you happy in Melchester?'

Rocky felt like she'd woken up from a long sleep. The air was so fresh and the wind roaring in her ears. She felt a little more alive than she had for weeks.

*I'm not happy in Melchester*, she said to herself. It was like a lightning bolt. *I have lived here all my life and it has been normal and just... just that's how it is... and now I am questioning it. I've seen my best friend move to America. I've flown to another country. For the first time. I've seen other places. I've felt how it feels to get away.*

'No,' she said.

'What?'

Roy had said it too loud. The deer looked at them for a half-second, its nostrils wide. Then it bolted, crashing through the bushes and trees.

They both listened and then – when they could hear only the wind – Roy frowned.

'I'm not always happy here. In Melchester.'

'But what do you want? Where would you go?'

That was when Rocky Race had the epiphany that would change the game, her life, change everything.

'Somewhere else.' Rocky was smiling. 'Maybe not today, tomorrow. But some day I would like to be somewhere else, see what it's like to live away from here.'

Rocky could feel her heart pounding faster. Like a drum thumping inside her. A drum that signalled change was coming. Change she wanted.

**6**

HAVING TOLD ROY that she wanted to move away from Melchester, Rocky remembered last year thinking she wanted to join the Army. And how – in the past – she had come up with other plans that would mean a big change. She thought again about Ffion and how she had left Melchester, left England and gone on to live a life most people could only dream of. In America.

Sitting on the rocks now, where you could look across the city and down the valley, Rocky stared at the lights of the city beneath them.

Her city.

Melchester.

Looking at those lights and how the motorway and railway tracks led out of Melchester and into the hills, then at the flightpath of aeroplanes taking off, then turning south, she understood something. Something she didn't dare think through too far it was so painful.

'What do you want?' Roy asked again, breaking into her thoughts.

The deer had gone now. It wasn't coming back. Rocky missed the silence she felt inside herself when she saw a deer or a fox. That sense of being near a wild animal that made you worry less about yourself and think instead about the deer or fox. It occurred to her that she had not seen a fox for months. She wondered if they still even lived in Melchester.

Remembering that Roy had asked her a question, Rocky turned to her brother.

'I want to leave Melchester,' she told him.

Silence.

Rocky studied her brother. His mouth was wide open and in his eyes she could see that he just didn't understand, didn't have it in him.

To want to leave Melchester?

It would never occur to him.

She almost laughed. But she didn't. This wasn't a time for laughing. And it would be rude. Her brother loved their city. And so did she. But not like him. For Roy, Melchester was everything and he was proud to have lived every day of his life here.

But Rocky wanted something different.

She smiled to herself. What was happening to her? She was trying not to be rude to Roy. What was this? Her life's work was to wind him up. Now she was protecting him from her harsh thoughts.

Then Roy said the thing that she hadn't wanted to think about. The thing she was constantly avoiding.

'What about Mum?' he asked.

And there it was. The big question. Rocky stared hard at the hills beyond the city, where the long-set sun was creating a dark silhouette to the west. Of hills. A sense of being trapped, stifled. A sense of claustrophobia.

What about Mum?

What about her?

Mum. A widow for a few weeks, living with her seventeen-year-old daughter and nineteen-year-old son. A woman with no husband after twenty years of happy marriage. Without the man she'd expected to live long with, retire with, wake up with every morning. And here was Rocky thinking that the thing she most wanted in the world was to get away from that, leave her mum on her own.

Urgh.

Rocky said nothing. There was nothing to say.

Then she felt her brother's hand on her shoulder.

She wanted to pull away from his touch, but didn't. She just sat there rigid until he took his hand away. She hated being touched by other people. But she knew he meant to be supportive, so she tolerated it. For once.

She sighed again.

'Where do you want to go?' Roy asked.

Rocky could tell he was embarrassed, uncomfortable. Here was the Melchester Rovers legend, loved by all, lost for words. Not sure if he should put his arm round his sister, ask her questions or just shut up. And the worst thing was that Rocky didn't have the words or the will to say anything to comfort him.

Rocky shrugged. 'I dunno,' she said, standing up.

Roy stared up at her as a blast of wind struck Rocky. He tried to get up, but his foot slipped on the rock and he stumbled.

'Careful there, old timer,' Rocky laughed. 'Do you need a little help?'

She put her hand out. Roy took it and eased himself up.

Then he smiled and Rocky knew they were okay.

'You don't really want to talk about it, do you?' Roy asked.

'I just did,' Rocky objected.

'True.'

'But I've had enough now,' Rocky

admitted. 'Let's get home to Mum. She'll be wondering where we are.'

IT WAS QUIET when Roy parked Mum's car outside the small terraced house where they had lived their whole lives. No media. In fact, there was no one about. It could be three in the morning, even though it was only a little after ten p.m.

There were no lights on in the house.

'She must have gone to bed?' Rocky suggested.

She checked her phone. No text from Mum to say 'Night night' like there always was. Rocky felt a shiver of unease.

'Shall I text her?' Roy asked.

'We might wake her.'

They both went silent as a young fox walked impossibly along the top of a fence, balancing as its weight caused the fence to bend slightly.

Rocky grinned and – carefully – lifted her phone to film it. Then she decided not to film it, but to just watch it, enjoy it. It was enough that she liked that she'd seen a fox. Felt it was a good omen. A sign. A fox and a deer in one day. Although she wasn't quite sure what it was a sign of, she felt good, deep down, a glow of warmth inside.

Once the fox had gone, sister and brother climbed out of the car and shut the doors quietly. There was a faint drizzle drifting from the hills. Somehow it made the darkness of the street even darker.

Then they went inside the house. Quietly easing the front door open, so as not to wake Mum.

Rocky went into the kitchen, making sure not to put the strip light on because the buzz it made was loud enough to wake someone in the bedrooms above. She crept in, and saw the back door from the kitchen was open and that, outside, Mum was in the garden sitting on the two-seater bench, swirling a glass of wine in her hand, staring at the contents.

There was a bottle on the floor by her feet. Empty by the look of it.

Rocky felt her shoulders drop and an overwhelming ache somewhere deep inside her. There was a memory. Since they were tiny. Since she could remember. Mum and Dad sat on the bench outside, or the back step, having a glass of wine, a beer, a cup of tea as the sun went down, the soft sound of their voices and laughter – always laughter – drifting up through Rocky's back bedroom window. And Rocky not knowing what they were talking about, not caring. Just knowing they were there, together, her parents. And the thing that really got her now was that she always thought of her parents as one thing. Not two people, but one. It was hard to explain. Even to herself. But the sadness came from the fact that Mum was on her own in the dark with one glass of wine, not two, and that she was silent.

Roy was upstairs already, creeping

around, still assuming Mum was asleep in the front bedroom. Rocky blinked hard, grabbed a glass and filled it with tap water. Then she went to join Mum.

And something came to Rocky. She was nervous. Nervous that she didn't know what to do to help her mum. It was impossible. Mum was struggling. But Rocky was struggling too. Struggling to know how to help. So what could she do? How did you help someone who had lost her partner for life decades before that was supposed to happen?

Walking across the cobbles Rocky understood at least one thing.

Mum needed her.

Just like she'd needed Mum all those years as a child, the tables had turned now. Whatever that meant. Rocky wasn't sure what it meant literally, but she knew the phrase *tables have turned* meant that she needed to look after her mum now and that, maybe, she shouldn't expect her mum to look after her anymore. Not so much.

Rocky understood that there was one thing she could do. Something she would do. She had to suppress the excitement she'd felt on the Moor, the idea that she could leave Melchester.

She was stuck here. She had to stay. She had to put her hopes and dreams on hold.

THREE DAYS LATER Rocky was on the pitch, thinking about nothing but the game, the ball, where it was and where it was going. Not even thinking about the fact that Mum never came to watch her play anymore. She hadn't come to either Roy's or Rocky's games since Dad had died. Said she found it overwhelming.

And that was fine.

Melchester Rovers were playing against the strongest opposition yet. A tough opponent and a tough game. As Rocky climbed off the floor after another sliding tackle, she wondered if the match would end 0–0. She'd

109

never ever played in a goalless game and –
because it was her job to shield the defence,
even drop back to hoover up behind the
defence – she kind of wanted it to end 0–0.
There was something delicious about a game
without goals for a player like her.

'I want you to play as the libero,' Serina
Heracles instructed Rocky.

Rocky understood. They had practised
libero in training.

The libero was an old-fashioned position,
a tactic that was popular more than fifty
years before. She was a midfielder who
played behind the defence and received the
ball, who would then move forward, through
her defenders, to play the ball to the wings
or through the pitch. Constantly involved in
defence – and in attack.

'So you want me to attack?' Rocky had
asked.

Heracles nodded. 'I want you to attack. And I want you to defend.'

Another attack from Wakefield United, who played fast-paced attacking football with lots of close passing in midfield. Rocky tracked the two forwards, trying to give them 100% of her attention.

She had worked out how the Wakefield duo operated. One would take the ball, shield it, play it to the other, then take it back again and that would open up the Melchester Rovers defence.

But not if Rocky read it right.

Confident her centre backs – Eve Ainsworth and Emma Aluko – were right behind her, as soon as forward one played the ball to forward two, Rocky would close down the first aggressively and at pace, making their move impossible, ending with Eve or Emma mopping up the ball.

Then, with Rocky having dropped back, she would receive the ball, then make a run forward, with the opposition still out of position.

The tactic having worked again, Rocky drove forward, through her defence and past the breathless opposition forwards. She saw two of her teammates calling for the pass.

Yamile Hernandez, calling for a through-ball, running towards the penalty area. Narinder Mehmi, wide on the left in loads of space, pointing for a weighted pass ahead of her.

Rocky was surprised that no one had tackled her yet. She had run with the ball into the centre circle, unhassled. She remembered what her coach had said to her.

*They won't expect this form of play. We can surprise them.*

Rocky took two more paces, nudging the ball ahead of her, then, just as she saw the opposition defence move forward as one, trying to play Yamile and Priscilla offside, Rocky slid a ball through the opposition midfield and defence, like a knife through butter.

And there was Priscilla. Onto the ball. One touch. Two touches, drawing the keeper out, then hitting it low and hard.

The net shook. Drops of rainwater showering onto the Wakefield United keeper, who lay in a heap, crestfallen.

1–0.

Melchester were beating a good team 1–0. A really good team.

For the rest of the second half the opposition pressed higher and higher, forcing Melchester Rovers back. And it was hard. There was no space for Rocky to play the libero role. The opposition coach had instructed her two strikers to close Rocky down as soon as the ball was at her feet.

It was a struggle, but she tried to keep to her brief. Like her teammates. And it felt good that – even though they were under pressure – Rocky always had options. There were always two or even three other Melchester Rovers players there to take a pass from her.

Then – at last – the final whistle. A 1–0 victory against a team that would have beaten them 6–0 the year before.

Something special happened after the game. Something that made Rocky feel different. After the opposition players had congratulated Rocky and her teammates, Serina Heracles brought her squad into a group, where the players stood in a tight circle looking into each other's eyes, listening to their coach.

It wasn't so much the words their coach said, but the looks on the faces of her teammates. It seemed like their eyes were sparkling as they looked at each other. And Rocky felt something she'd not felt before. An intensity. Of being in a team. Of footballers she trusted. Of friends. It was a bit like... what was it a bit like?

And then Rocky got it. It was a bit like nothing she had ever felt. It was new and it was now. And she liked it.

AFTER SHOWERING AND getting dressed, Rocky and Yamile were walking and talking, heading in the direction of the car park. Talking the goal through. Yamile Hernandez was the only Melchester Rovers player who was not British. Everyone else was from England, Scotland or Wales.

Yamile was American. And this was exciting for Rocky.

Rocky liked having an American in the team for a reason. USA were the best football team in the world and to have a USA player on the team made Rocky feel like they were going somewhere. Like they were aiming high.

'You should have played it to me,' Yamile joked.

'Sorry, Yamile. Next time?'

'You promise?'

'No.'

The two players laughed, arm in arm, as the opposition coach approached them to shake their hands.

Helen White. Famous for scoring the winning goal in the FA Cup final twenty years ago.

White held onto Rocky's hand for a little longer than Rocky was used to. They looked into each other's eyes. Then White nodded.

'You won't be in Melchester for long, Rocky Race,' White said.

Rocky – confused by what the Wakefield coach had meant – just smiled and said thank you. And the exchange was over.

'What was that?' Priscilla said, coming up behind Rocky and Yamile.

Rocky shrugged.

Yamile took up the story. 'So she stops Rocky and says she won't be in Melchester forever. Like some sort of fortune teller or something or one of those characters who pop up in one of your Shakespeare plays. It was amazing.'

Rocky shoved Yamile, knocking her sideways. She felt embarrassed. But she knew it had been a compliment. A woman who had scored the winner in the FA Cup final had made a point to tell Rocky that she had a future in football. Maybe that was what she had meant?

Amazing. Rocky was buzzing. Almost as much as when she played that ball through to Priscilla to see her shot slam against the back of the net.

Out of the stadium and into the car park outside reception, they saw them. Cameras. More cameras. And a huddle of journalists. The same ones who'd been trying to follow Roy and Rocky the night they'd gone up to the Moor.

Then came the questions. Flung at them. But not even like they were expecting an answer. They felt more like insults.

'Did you stay on the pitch for the whole ninety today, girls?'

'Got a bit more balls than the men, then, eh?'

'They're goading us,' Priscilla muttered. 'Trying to get a rise. Just ignore them.'

'No racism today, girls?'

Rocky watched Priscilla and Yamile glare at the journalists as more questions came. She frowned, but did what her senior teammates were doing by trying not to react.

'They're still going on about the Spartak thing,' Priscilla said. 'They're trying to get someone to say something that they can create a story around.'

'The media in the US are just as bad,' Yamile added. 'It's like when people say stuff and ask stuff on social media. Fishing for something, anything. To make money out of it.'

Rocky and the rest of the team walked on to the car park.

'Say nothing,' Yamile whispered to Rocky. 'Don't react and give them something to write about. If you say something good, they won't print it. If you say anything bad, they'll take it out of context.'

They'd ignore the journalists. They wouldn't give the gutter press anything to write about. Passive. They'd be passive. Rocky knew that she was being coached by the senior players not to lose her temper.

And she would do as they asked. She wanted to learn from her teammates on and off the pitch.

Then another question.

'You look more like the United Nations than Melchester Rovers.'

Rocky stopped. The other girls stopped too.

Priscilla stepped forward. 'What do you mean?' she asked the journalist in a calm voice. Cameras flashed, the photographers hoping for an inflammatory moment.

Rocky saw only blank faces on the journalists. One of them had asked the question, but no one owned up to it now. But, whoever had asked it, Rocky knew it wasn't meant well. Why would you say that? *You look more like the United Nations than Melchester Rovers?* Rocky turned it over in her mind. She knew. She understood. The journalist was saying that the team had players from diverse backgrounds. That they weren't all white.

So what? Rocky wondered. What did it even matter? Why comment on that?

Rocky frowned. What was it about football? There was always someone trying to make trouble or make money or make a point. Always something under the surface that was so slippery she could never quite grasp it.

Why couldn't people just mind their own business and be nice?

'Come on,' Priscilla said. 'Let's go.'

BACK HOME FROM the football, Rocky sat with Mum and they watched *Strictly* together. Glitzy costumes, jazzy music and kind-hearted banter filling the room with something that felt like happiness. That's what TV shows like *Strictly* and *Bake Off* did. They took you away from your worries and showed you people being – on the whole – kind to each other.

Rocky got that.

She didn't particularly like dance, but she still loved *Strictly* because of its vibe. That and the fact it was something she had always watched with Mum over the years. Every year of her life probably.

Sometimes it made her feel emotional. All that intensity. Sometimes her eyes would well up. She would hide it, but she knew, for years, her mum had seen the reaction, but never reacted. Rocky loved Mum all the more for that.

There was something else about *Strictly* too. It was about how the celebrities who did well were open to improving. They would listen to the judges and try to do what they were told to improve on.

Just like being a footballer.

Identify your weaknesses. Work on them. Improve.

Find new weaknesses. Work on them. Improve.

Week after week.

Month after month.

Year after year.

Rocky got that too. And she felt, as a result, like she'd learned a lot. For the football. If there was anything that could help her to improve her football, she would buy into it.

Rocky also knew that *Strictly* was something her mum loved: the two of them watching the dance. Guessing the scores the panel would give. Laughing. Sometimes crying. But crying about other people's lives, not their own. Living through other people's dramas. That was better than constantly thinking about your own dramas, wasn't it?

Watching the show, Mum smiling to herself, Rocky had an idea. An advert had come up about a live *Strictly* show where you could actually go and see the dancers perform in arenas around the UK.

What about taking Mum to see that? Or

something like that? Something they could do together as daughter and mother. Maybe not the big show, Rocky reflected, if Mum didn't want to be in the crowds at the football.

But something else. Like what? A day out. What did Mum like? A meal out? What did people do together? Adults? A trip somewhere. Shopping? No, Rocky hated shopping. A city break? Hmmm. There must be something.

Heading upstairs after *Strictly*, Rocky felt good. She'd spent time with her mum. Her mum seemed happy. And Rocky had had an idea for something for the future: something for Mum to look forward to. And – for a while – Rocky knew that she would feel okay about Mum. About their lives. About herself.

In her room, watching WSL highlights, Rocky saw she had an incoming FaceTime.

Rocky felt her heart leap as Ffion's name appeared on the screen.

Her old teammate looked different.

Was it her hair? Probably.

Or make-up. Or maybe something else.

Rocky couldn't work it out. Maybe living in California, going to Steinbeck University, was changing her friend. It was bound to change her. Again, Rocky had that wild fantasy that she could do the same. Just fly away and leave England. And there she was again, wishing she could abandon Mum. That thought again. That feeling of betrayal. Rocky felt like she was being torn in two.

'Great result today,' Ffion said, breaking into her thoughts.

'I know,' Rocky grinned, excited that Ffion – who was thousands of miles away in the United States – was aware how Melchester had got on.

'And have you heard the news about who you're playing in a couple of weeks?' Ffion asked.

'Dunno. I take every game as it comes,' Rocky said, knowing she sounded like one of the players being interviewed after the game on *Match of the Day*. 'Who?'

'Us.'

'What?'

'Us! You're playing us. We're coming over for a friendly. A little tour of the UK. And our first game is Melchester Rovers. Can you believe it?'

Rocky couldn't. 'No way. This is ace. Oh my God! And I'll get to see you. And Roy will too. This is fab…'

'It's a secret for now,' Ffion told her, grinning. 'I think your coach is going to tell your teammates soon. But I couldn't wait to tell you.'

Rocky's mind moved on a notch. To the game.

'Are you good? I mean… how good are you? Will you batter us?'

'We'll try,' Ffion answered. And Rocky caught that steely look in her old teammate's eye.

Rocky inhaled. 'You'll have to get through me first,' she muttered. 'And my new teammates.'

'I was looking at the team sheet, actually,' Ffion said. 'It's changed, hasn't it?'

'Yeah. New players. Lots of them.'

Rocky had noticed that Ffion's accent had changed. Just a bit. It was hard to tell how. But some of the ways she said certain words sounded different. It was weird. She was seeing new things in Ffion immediately after she had said they were to play against each other. Ffion was a rival now as well as a friend.

'They all okay?' Ffion asked.

'Who?'

'The new Mel players?'

'Yeah. Great. Lily's still in goal. She survived the changes after you left.'

'So are you two the only English players left?' Ffion pressed.

Rocky shook her head. 'No. I was just thinking that. Someone from the press said something similar just now. Outside the ground. But we have one American, Yamile Hernandez, and the rest are all British, I'm pretty sure. Not like some of the big teams in the WSL.'

'They don't sound it. Danquah. Pielichaty. Aluko. Really?'

'Yeah,' Rocky smiled, proud of her teammates. 'I mean, Helena's dad was Polish or something. And I think Priscilla's family is from Barbados. But generations back. I dunno.' Rocky laughed. 'It doesn't matter, anyway? Does it?'

A silence from Ffion. She hadn't moved.

Rocky touched the screen. Was the connection going down?

'It'd be good to keep some British players in the team, though,' Ffion insisted. 'Don't you reckon? I mean, what happens when they get rid of you and Lily Halifax? Even your coach is a foreigner.'

Rocky shrugged. She wanted to reiterate that all the players were British, except Yamile. And to say that it didn't matter anyway. But she found herself clamming up. She wasn't sure what was going on. Ffion had never said stuff like this when she lived in the UK. Her brother – Vic, who played with Roy for the men – could be a bit random, but not Ffion. Maybe living in the States was changing her. Did you change when you went to a new country? Did you change when you changed all your friends in one great sweep?

Another silence. All the excitement Rocky had felt about playing Ffion's university team had passed.

'At Steinbeck we're got a squad of twenty-four and only two are foreigners. A Mexican and a girl from Ghana. The rest are white.'

'Right,' Rocky said. She was panicking. She wanted to shut the screen down and hide because she was so confused about what Ffion was saying. And what it meant.

American? British? Foreign? White? Was this for real? Rocky was finding it hard to think straight, to process her thoughts. Was Ffion right? Or were her instincts right that something was wrong? It was so confusing. She just couldn't process all of this in her mind.

Rocky was really troubled. She wanted to call her friend out, like her coach had said, but how did you do that? How did you call out one of the people you like and respect most in the world for saying something that was racist?

Because that's what she felt was happening. Ffion was being racist.

Rocky had no idea. Her head was all over the place.

In a panic, Rocky made a decision.

She started a sentence, knowing she wouldn't finish it, her hand hovering on the END CALL button. She had done this before. Just felt like she didn't want to talk to anyone anymore and knowing she could just stop it with the flick of a finger and blame it on the Wifi.

'Anyway,' she said, trying to sound excited and not like she was about to do what she was about to do, 'I wanted to tell you about our new coach and…'

Rocky pressed the button to end the call and tossed the phone to the foot of her bed. And now her hands were on her face in the silence of her small bedroom, rain lashing against the window.

*You should have called her out*, Rocky said to herself.

No answer.

And – like she always did when she was unhappy with the way a conversation had gone – she began to rerun the conversation, thinking of better things she could have said. Trying desperately to process it all. Assailed by questions questions questions.

*They don't sound English. Danquah. Pielichaty. Aluko. Really?*

What was that Ffion had said? And what had it meant? That her teammates at Melchester didn't have English names? What was an English name supposed to be? Smith? Jones? Butcher? Baker? Candlestickmaker?

Rocky wondered if she would have dared say that. Or just say something like, Ffion, there are loads of people from all over the world in England who are English. Your name? Ffion Guthrie. Is that English? It sounds a bit Irish or Welsh to me.

Would she say that to her hero?

No.

She wished she could.

Why couldn't she?

Urgh. Rocky picked up the plastic mug at the side of her bed and flung it across the room. It bounced off the wall, the handle snapping off.

Rocky felt immediately better.

She heard Mum shout up, 'Are you all right, love?'

'Yeah,' Rocky called down. 'Dropped something.'

Rocky listened out for her mum. No more questions.

*At Steinbeck we're got a squad of twenty-four and only two are foreigners. A Mexican and a girl from Ghana. The rest are white.*

Is that what Ffion had said?

Yes, that was it.

Rocky had a great reply for that one. Even though the call had ended minutes ago.

Three foreigners, she would have said. Three. There's you too, Ffion. You're foreign in the USA. You're British. And what difference does it make being white?

*That would have been a good reply*, Rocky thought.

But would she have said it? Would she have dared challenge the person she most admired in the world after her mum? Would she dare call out anyone?

Clearly not. She had not done so. Serina Heracles would have been disappointed.

Rocky swore and pulled her duvet over her face as the conversation went round and round her head, with the things she'd said and hadn't said swirling around her mind.

That night she slept terribly.

ROCKY WAS BACK at Mel Park. But this time she was in the stands, not on the pitch. At a men's game.

When she came to watch the men's games now she always felt this way.

Different.

Because everything had changed in so few months for Rocky. She had gone from being a 100% devoted home fan of Melchester Rovers Men, from considering the men's team part of her DNA, from sitting in these red and yellow seats close to the pitch, to something very different.

For Rocky, being a Melchester Rovers fan was the second most important thing in her life. No longer the first.

The first was now being a Melchester Rovers footballer.

'And I can't get my head round the grass anymore,' she said to herself.

But aloud.

Embarrassed, Rocky looked to either side of her. On her left, Helena. On her right, Priscilla. Her two favourite teammates sitting in Roy's seat and Mum's seat. Both looking at her with quizzical expressions on their faces.

'Erm...?'

'Yes, Rocky... and thanks again for giving us your tickets, by the way. This is ace. I can't believe we're at a National Cup quarter final.'

'You're welcome,' Rocky smiled, 'but

doesn't it feel weird to you, now, that the grass is over there and we're used to being on it?'

'Not really,' Priscilla admitted.

As the men's team came on to warm up, Rocky felt a rush of energy. The kind she had before a game. That she could use to play well, play with the intensity she needed.

'And do you have loads of adrenaline?' she asked her teammates. 'So much so that you can't help wishing you could run on the pitch?'

'Not really,' Helena replied this time. 'In fact, it's nice to put our feet up. Let the boys put a shift in and we can just shout at them. We can relax.'

Rocky frowned and sat back in her seat. That was the opposite of what she felt. Feet up? Relax? That wasn't her style. But soon the noise from the crowd overwhelmed her and she felt herself shift from wannabe player to fan.

Then she remembered what Helena had said. This was a National Cup quarter final. A HUGE game. And here she was in player mode. She should forget all that and get behind the team. Back to fan mode. It was so confusing. She would just have to behave like a fan again and it would come back.

'Rovers! Rovers! Rovers!' she joined in with a chant from the main stand, trying to get into the mood.

Her two friends stared at her. They looked shocked.

'What?' Rocky asked.

'Er... nothing,' Priscilla said.

And then it clicked. The way Priscilla and Helena had not known what to do with their tickets at the gate. The way they had been surprised when someone under the stand had started singing a song alone and several people had joined in. Then the way they gasped coming out into the stadium seats.

'Have neither of you been to a match at Mel Park before?' Rocky shouted above the chant that she had started in their stand. *Rovers! Rovers! Rovers!* Rolling round the stands.

Both shook their heads.

'Not like this!' Priscilla shouted. 'Not so many fans. A big team. And it's all so positive and happy... not like at Spartak. It's... amazing.'

Now Rocky felt proud. Her friends were not Mel Rovers fans. They'd not been brought up on a diet of sitting in the stands, watching the game before playing it. They were doing it the other way round. Now Rocky felt like she had a purpose. To show them how it was done.

She started a chant. Slow at first, hoping others would join in.

*One team in Melchester!*
*There's only one team in Melchester!*

The song took hold and rippled through the stand. Not the rest of the stadium, but at least five thousand had been singing it. And Rocky could see her two friends were impressed.

THE GAME BEGAN. The quarter final of the National Cup. Melchester Rovers against Everpool. The winner was going to Wembley for a semi-final.

It was the first time the men's team had played top flight opposition in the cup this year. It was a test. A proper test. Rocky could tell from the Everpool players how much fitter and stronger they were as individuals. They were so fit up close, from their movement to their body fat ratio, that they seemed like science experiments. She had always thought her brother and his teammates looked fit. But compared to the top flight team, Melchester looked like boys against men.

And yet.

And yet... Rocky couldn't help thinking, however fit they looked, they also looked like they weren't giving it everything.

Then Helena – as if she'd been listening into Rocky's thoughts – gave a reason why.

'They reckon the Everpool manager has lost the dressing room. I mean... they don't look like they're playing for him, do they?'

It was true. The Everpool players were shirking tackles and rolling their eyes when the manager called out instructions.

'They're playing to get him sacked,' Priscilla added. 'They've lost their last three games in the league and now this…'

Rocky rubbed her hands with glee. Were they on for a cup shock? Maybe.

Ten minutes later, the sacking of the Premier League coach looked more likely.

Vernon Elliott powered down the flank, turned and knocked the ball back to Lofty Peak, Roy screaming for a pass. Rocky watched as the ball was played long to her brother as he cut across the defensive line, to reach it, control it, take one touch, then suddenly have it whipped off his feet. But not by an opposition player. It was Jimmy Slade, barrelling through the defence himself, taking the ball off Roy, knocking him to the ground, then hitting it at the goal.

The roar from the fans was deafening.

Rocky, not really understanding who had hit it, but knowing it was a goal, leaped from her seat and grabbed a confused Helena, then Priscilla.

1–0.

Rocky stopped celebrating to see Jimmy Slade mobbed by his teammates, then Roy on his own on the edge of the penalty area, rubbing his thigh.

'Oh Jimmy Jimmy… Jimmy Jimmy Jimmy Jimmy Jimmy Slade,' the crowd roared.

Then 'Premier League? You're having a laugh' echoing into the darkening sky.

When the replay came up on the big screen, there was a murmuring from the crowd. Rocky knew what was going on. Fans were talking about how the goal was Roy's to score, but that Jimmy had whipped it off his feet, even barged him off the ball.

She was happy they were winning. But

not about what Slade had done to Roy. She could sense the rest of the fans were a bit confused about it too.

1–0 at half time and into the second half. Rocky decided not to talk about how she was annoyed. The stolen goal was not the only thing. Throughout the first and now this half Slade was trying to boss the game, calling out defenders as if he was the captain. And calling for balls that should be going to Roy. Rocky noticed these things now. And one thing she could definitely see was that it was getting to Roy. His game was off.

The next incident that made her angry came with less than ten minutes to go. Roy took the ball from Asif Mirza and started to run directly at the Everpool defence. He – like Rocky – had clocked that they didn't like it. That they were tackle-shy, didn't like people running at them, weren't sure how to cope with it. Roy took it from the edge of the centre circle to the edge of the D before he was clipped by an Everpool midfielder backtracking.

There was a howl from the crowd as Roy tumbled and took a breath on the pitch. Then a sharp shrill whistle. Melchester Rovers Men had been awarded a direct free kick in range of goal.

Several shouts from the crowd. 'Give it the Rocket, Roy!' 'Come on, Roy, you can bury it from there.'

But Jimmy Slade had collected the ball and was standing over it, pushing his teammates away.

Rocky saw her brother walk over to Slade to take the ball. Roy took the free kicks from the right. That was the agreement. His left foot could do the most damage.

But not this time.

Slade grabbed the ball, pushed Roy away and placed it.

'Seriously?' Rocky shouted.

Then chaos. Mayhem. Sometimes there wasn't a word for her anger. Just something in her head. That thing again.

She jumped to her feet and moved to get past Helena. There was no way she was going to let Jimmy Slade take Roy's free kick. Who did this joker think he was?

Out of the seats, she stormed down the steps. Three at a time, ankles jarring, while shouting and pointing. Rocky hit the cinder track that surrounded the pitch, then – hearing footsteps and the roar of the crowd – ran to jump over the advertising hoardings. Remembering hurdles from school, she gathered speed and leaped over the hoarding.

Grass under her feet now. The glare of

light on the pitch. Was she going to do this?
Was she going to invade the pitch? What
happened if you did that?

And – as she hesitated – Rocky felt
someone grab her and pull her back. A man's
hands on her coat. She felt it begin to rip and

tried to release her arms from the coat, but whoever it was had her tight. She saw a flash of orange. A steward.

Rocky shouted, 'No!' Then something rude.

Two people were holding her now. One male, one female. Both bigger than her. Stronger.

'Get off the pitch, Rocky, you idiot!' the woman shouted. 'You'll get banned. Just come with us.'

Rocky was led through the tunnel and under the stand where she was given a severe talking to.

'We should chuck you out!'

Then the woman looked Rocky in the eyes. 'If we let you go back, you have to promise not to do it again.'

Rocky agreed.

'If you do it again, we'll be fired. Got it?'

Rocky nodded. 'I get it. I won't do it again,' she said. She felt calmer now. She knew this was madness. She was angry. But why? It was on her brother's behalf. She felt defensive of him. And it wasn't like a ripple of anger, a tremor. It was like an earthquake, something she couldn't stop. And she knew that – if the stewards had not stopped her – she would have run onto the pitch and God knows what would have happened then. To her career, even. To everything. If you were a player and you invaded the pitch as a fan, they'd have to punish you. Proper punish you.

When the two stewards let her go, Rocky said thank you and went back to her friends. It was hard to believe they were going to let her stay and watch. But they did. And she would keep her word. She would not do it again. Not get them into trouble. She owed them.

She slumped into her seat, head down.

Helena put her hand on Rocky's arm. 'You good now?'

Rocky nodded. 'I'm good. Trust me.'

Rocky kept her head down so she didn't have to see Jimmy Slade or the forlorn look on Roy's face. Any more of that and she'd be trying to get on the pitch again.

Now she started to ask herself questions.

This anger towards Jimmy Slade? Where had that come from?

Rocky heard the ref's whistle. Someone shouting, 'Go on, Jimmy. Bury it.' Then a thump of a ball being struck and the roar of a stadium full of fans celebrating a goal that meant a certain victory.

But Rocky wasn't celebrating. She had her head down. She was staring at the concrete floor beneath her feet. What was happening to her? Why was she so confused? Not celebrating goals? Feeling like she didn't even want to be there?

And then – as she sat staring at her feet, the stadium celebrating almost certain qualification for the semi-finals of the National Cup – she remembered something.

Dad.

Danny Race was the most mild-mannered calm man you could meet. When he'd lost his job he'd been calm. When his mum – Rocky's gran – had died suddenly he'd been calm. When Rocky had burned down the garden shed by accident? Calm also.

Dad was always calm and kind.

Except when he was at the football. Her dad could really lose it when he was at the football. Rocky thought it through. When Dad was under pressure at work or home he would be calm, but at the football around that time, he'd go crazy. That was his emotional release. That was where he could let himself go. That was what football was for him.

Rocky smiled. She was like her dad. That felt good. That felt very good. That would do for now.

And she knew now that she wasn't angry with Jimmy Slade. Not really. It was just that she could be angry with him when she couldn't be angry with Mum for being lonely or Dad for being dead.

And with Ffion. Rocky was angry with Ffion too. But – unlike with her anger at Mum and Dad – there was something she could do with her anger at Ffion.

ROCKY HEADED HOME immediately after the
final whistle.

Helena offered her a lift, but Rocky liked
to walk with the fans in streams away from
the ground as they made their way into the
pubs or along the ring road then up into the
estates and lines of terraced houses to the
east of the city.

Most people drove to the football now,
filling car parks and the roads around the
stadium with traffic and exhaust fumes. But
not so the fans who lived nearby. Rocky liked
that she was one of them. Local. Very local.

And as she walked – surrounded by so many other fans – she always felt safe. She didn't always feel safe walking home alone in the dark. But post-match she didn't really feel like she was alone. These were her people.

But as she walked among the familiar streets in the post-match calm and satisfaction of a win, Rocky couldn't stop feeling vexed with Jimmy and anxious about Ffion.

People.

All these other people and the things they did and said.

Why did it have to affect her so much? Why did Jimmy being selfish have to stop her really enjoying the men's team winning? Why did what Ffion had said make her less excited about playing football against an American team?

Urgh. Life. Why was it so unsettled and so unsettling?

Rocky was looking forward to getting home and talking to Mum. Mum would help her out. For a while now, Rocky had been keeping her worries and traumas to herself, sometimes talking to Roy, but not so much to Mum.

Was that because of Dad being ill?

Probably.

Or maybe it was something else. Maybe there had come a time when she had stopped going to her mum with the things that troubled her. Since she'd turned seventeen maybe she'd thought Mum couldn't help her. Maybe that was it.

Rocky picked up her pace going up the hill. Head down, wondering what she'd say to her mum. About Ffion. Because that was what had been worrying her. Rocky smiled. She knew Mum could help her. That she'd have an answer, a way of looking at the problem.

Rocky tried to rehearse what she'd say to Mum. *I think Ffion was racist and it made me feel uncomfortable. That she said what she said, but that I didn't call her out.*

Something like that?

Yes. Something like that.

Rocky reached the front door. Opened it. From the hallway she could hear the TV. Mum was watching the news.

'Hi, Mum. We won two–nil.'

'Great, love. Well done.'

Mum sounded distant. It was weird she'd said well done too. Had she even thought Rocky had been playing, not the men's team?

Rocky smiled.

She put her hand on the banister to steady herself as she slid her trainers off and felt the banister rock as she put her weight on it. It felt a bit loose. Dad would have to fix it or it might break off.

Rocky closed her eyes and paused. Another of those Dad thoughts. Dad will do this. Dad can get that. Not anymore. Dad wouldn't be doing any of that. So who would?

She would. That was who. She was good at DIY. She'd put that mirror up last year, hadn't she? And Dad did use to teach her DIY stuff when he was able to. She'd see to it tomorrow.

Determined to talk to Mum about Ffion, Rocky went in to see her.

'Cup of tea?' Rocky asked, peering in to see Mum with an empty dinner plate on the low coffee table in front of the sofa.

Dinner plate?

She must have eaten her dinner at least three hours ago. That was weird. Why hadn't she cleared it away? She always cleared dishes away as soon as they'd finished eating.

Rocky took the plate into the kitchen.

It was unusually cold in there and Rocky realised that one of the windows was slightly open, letting cold air in. But the heating was on! That was weird too. Mum would never have a door or window open if the heating was on. Never.

Rocky shrugged, made two cups of tea and headed in to join Mum. Some adverts were on. TV adverts were weird, Rocky thought. They just looked so old-fashioned now.

Rocky sat down.

'Can I switch the TV off, Mum? There's something I need to ask you about.'

Mum picked up her mug and blew across the surface of the tea, a puff of steam disappearing into the air.

'Yes, love,' Mum said. 'I wasn't watching it, anyway.'

Rocky frowned, but decided not to

challenge her to say she had been watching it. Maybe she'd been asleep. Maybe it didn't matter.

'I had this conversation with Ffion,' Rocky said, wanting to talk it through before Roy got home, when her mum would jump up and make him a hot drink, fix him a sandwich. Probably.

No reaction. Mum was still staring at the empty TV screen.

'Mum?'

'Yes, love.'

'I was talking to Ffion and...'

Mum looked confused. 'Is she back from America?'

'No, no,' Rocky shook her head. 'Well, not yet, but she is...'

'Oh, that's great. For good? Is she coming home?'

'No. Just for a match. Against us. But

that's not what I wanted to tell you about. There's this thing. This stupid thing. And it's doing my head in.' Rocky tried to explain. 'We did FaceTime and she... well, she said something funny... not funny... I mean, she said something I thought was racist and...'

Rocky studied Mum's face. There was no expression on it, except for a faint smile. This was the point that she would have expected Mum to sit forward and say something like: *Okay... calm down. Tell me everything... let's work it out.*

But she was just smiling, nodding.

It wasn't Mum.

Rocky felt a sudden choke of panic. That Dad wasn't here to fix the banister and now Mum wasn't here either. Not really here.

'And I don't know what to do,' Rocky said.

Silence.

'What shall I do?' Rocky tried again. 'Do I call her out?'

Mum looked at Rocky. 'I don't know, love,' she said.

Rocky frowned.

Mum smiled and placed her hand on Rocky's knee. Her voice was quiet, but firm.

'I can't even put my own dishes away, love,' she said. 'I can't even be bothered to get up and close the curtains or the window even though it's dark. I can't think about anything without my head stopping me, and me feeling like I am tangled up in a spider's web, something like that. Can't you ask your brother? He loves Ffion, doesn't he? Roy will know what to do.'

Rocky stared out of the window, the street lights coming in through the darkness outside. She'd missed that too. The curtains not drawn. The kitchen window. The dinner plate.

Rocky glanced at Mum.

Mum was staring at her.

'Mum?'

'I know you're asking for my help,' Mum gasped, as if she was struggling for air to breathe. 'But I think I need your help, love.'

Rocky felt like she'd been punched in the chest. She leaned forward, desperate not to show a reaction. And then Mum was crying, tears streaming down her face, wetting her top. A sudden and unexpected torrent.

For a half-second Rocky had no idea what to do. Just a half-second. Then she shuffled next to her mum and grabbed her, hugging her hard, feeling her mum sobbing now, trying to get her breath between the sobs, like she was drowning.

What now?

Rocky had no idea. Like that night she and Roy had come home and found Mum in the garden with her empty bottle of wine and in the dark. She had not known what to do to help then.

What was going on?

Rocky had to break things down to work out what was going on. Then she could help Mum.

Mum was crying. Sitting in the dark. Drinking. Mum couldn't help her or offer her advice. Mum was broken. Mum wasn't Mum.

Problems. Lots of problems and worries and questions.

And then – in a flash – the answer came to Rocky. Her mum was depressed. Her mum needed her. And the terrible truth was that she had been like this for weeks. And Rocky and Roy had been so absorbed by their own grief and their own worries on and off the football pitch that they had missed that all

Mum had was her grief and nothing else to think about, worry about, do, not do, places to go, anything.

Mum was still sobbing half an hour later when the door clicked and Roy came quietly in. Quiet because he would have been thinking that someone was asleep. He was thoughtful like that.

When he came into the front room, Roy saw Rocky and Mum hugging. Rocky's arms were hurting from hugging Mum so hard for so long.

'Hey,' Roy said softly, seeing the hug. 'What's up?'

Rocky frowned.

'Mum needs us,' she said. 'We have to help her.'

TRAINING. TWO DAYS later. The bliss of escaping into football and forgetting all the other things swirling round her head. But it wasn't that simple. Because, as Rocky put on her kit ready for a full training session, the events of that afternoon just gone went through her mind however much she tried to concentrate on football.


IT HAD BEEN an important day. For Mum. For all of them. Rocky had spent the morning with her. First up, as promised, calling the

171

GP, redialling and redialling and redialling until she got through to the receptionist, a man with an impossibly quiet voice.

It was the first time Rocky had called the GP for anyone. Even for herself. Any doctor's appointment she had ever had had been made by one of her parents. And here she was making one for her mum. It was like Rocky was the grown-up and Mum the child. How had that come about? It was one of those things that happens and you have to get used to quickly. Rocky was becoming increasingly aware of such things.

'Please can I have an appointment for my mum? Mrs Kathleen Race,' Rocky asked.

'Is she unable to make an appointment for herself?' the man whispered.

'Yes,' Rocky bristled.

Rocky knew she had to be polite. Firm, but polite. Her natural feeling was to be rude to the man, but that wouldn't help anyone. She knew that. She needed this man on her side, not against them.

'And why is that?' the receptionist asked.

Rocky felt another shiver of irritation. She knew the receptionist was just doing his job. But really? Did he need to ask such stupid questions?

'She is depressed,' Rocky replied.

'I see. Has she been diagnosed as depressed?'

Rocky sighed. She'd had enough. This man was being obstructive. And if he was going to be obstructive, she was going to be obstreperous. Rocky decided to give him the information he needed.

'Her husband – my dad – died a few weeks ago. That has made her extremely sad. I need an appointment because she is not eating. She sits in the same seat all day.

She is a danger to herself. I am worried about her mental health. If she had something equivalent relating to her physical health, I'd say she's lost a leg and is bleeding out.'

There had been a pause. Quite a long one.

'Right,' the man said. 'Forgive me, I have to ask those questions. It's like a script we have to follow. I apologise from the bottom of my heart for having to ask you those questions, especially after what your mum – and you – have suffered. Please forgive me. Now, can you bring her in?'

'Yes, I can.'

'Half-ten?'

'Perfect. Thank you.'

As she laced her boots, her mind back on training, Rocky felt a strange rush of emotion remembering how kind the receptionist had been on the phone in the end and how she felt bad about being so funny with him and how – when they actually visited the doctor's – they had looked after Mum like she was a VIP, like she was the most important patient they'd had in the surgery all year and that they were 100% in her corner.

Her eyes filled with tears and she rubbed them to hide her emotions. She caught Serina Heracles looking at her, briefly, then away.

Rocky shook her head and tried to focus.

'Think football,' she said to herself, standing, and ran out onto the outdoor training pitches, under the glare of the floodlights, fully illuminated even though it was only two in the afternoon. 'Think only football, football, football.'

Training began with a steady warm up. Then a training drill. The usual thing.

'Today,' Serina Heracles announced, 'the

drill is tackling. To gain possession. Or, at least, to take possession of the ball from the opponent.'

Rocky caught Coach glancing at her again. Had she seen Rocky looking emotional? Did she think she had been crying? She hadn't been crying, but maybe Serina Heracles would think she had. And she wondered how their new Dutch coach felt about her players blubbing. Did she see it like that? Did she see emotion as a weakness? Did she want her players to be hard in the tackle, hard in the mind? Rocky had no idea. She remembered that their last coach – Johnny Dexter, back with the men's team now – had a tough exterior, the toughest, but that, when it came to life and its vagaries, he was the most emotional person she knew.

'The opponent has the ball.' Serina Heracles was trying to articulate her plan for the drill. 'They have possession. This is a problem. Because we need the ball to score and to avoid being scored against. So, what can we do? We need to get the ball back. To do this we must tackle. Or we must press to force the error. Ideally in the opponent's half to create scoring opportunities. But tackling is not a job for one person. Pressing is not a job for one person. To win the ball we attack as a team, we also tackle as a team and press as a team. We are not alone.'

Rocky loved her new coach. She loved the way she made you think about football in a different way. If you'd asked her an hour ago to define tackling, Rocky would have said one player goes in and wins the ball off another by sticking their leg out. Something like that.

But not now. Not after this.

Rocky wondered sometimes if it was

because the coach was translating her words from Dutch to English. Did that make what she was saying clearer because it was simplified? She remembered in French at school they had done a play by an Irish author called Samuel Beckett and that he had written the play – *Waiting for Godot* – in French. And that he'd done so to make his meanings clearer and simpler. He'd even translated it back into English himself. Rocky had no idea where that memory had suddenly come from.

'Today we tackle in twos,' Heracles went on. 'One player presses, the other goes in for the ball. We close off the angles. We reduce the opponent's options from five things they can do down to one. And we make that one option so difficult, one time in three they lose the ball. Yes?'

'Yes,' the team repeated in unison.

Rocky joined up with Yamile and Emma. Closing down Eve Ainsworth, who was striding out of goal with the ball, with the intention of playing it to Charlotte Duncan.

They did the drill over and over. Again and again. Making it harder and harder for Eve and Charlotte. But with Eve and Charlotte finding ways to bamboozle them.

And then, suddenly, it was over. How had that happened? It was an hour and a half later and training was over. It felt like minutes to Rocky. Seconds even.

'Very good, ladies. Very good. Thank you for your focus, your time. Now, before we go to the dressing rooms, some news.'

The Melchester players stopped what they were doing and – in a sort of circle around their coach – stood ready to listen.

'We have an extra game coming next week. A friendly. We are to host the USA university, Steinbeck. They are on a short tour of the UK and one of their fixtures is to play us.'

There was something in the hubbub of voices that transmitted excitement to Rocky. The team were up for this. She tried her best to look surprised.

After their coach had explained everything, every player grabbed something to take back to the training store room. It was what they always did. But this time there was an electricity in the air. They were playing against an American university team! That was a big deal.

Rocky gathered balls in a large bag, her favourite thing to clear up after the game. There was something satisfying about gathering all the balls and slinging the bag over her shoulder, walking back to the dressing rooms. Usually last off.

But not today. Today she had Serina Heracles alongside her, carrying a stack of cones.

'Very good today, Rocky,' her coach said. 'You are improving week on week. Great progress.'

'Thanks, coach,' Rocky said, smiling at the compliment.

'How much training have you had before? Like proper drills, fitness, match practice. When did it begin for you?'

'A year ago,' Rocky said.

She heard Serina Heracles gasp.

'What?' Rocky smiled, embarrassed that she couldn't work out what the gasp had meant.

'You are seventeen. You have only played the game properly for a year. Under my training you are five times the better player than you were in just a few months. The world is at your feet, Rocky Race.'

Rocky was unsure what she meant. But she didn't want to fish for more compliments.

'I mean...' Heracles went on to fill the silence, 'the more you train the greater a footballer you will become. You can improve a hundred times if you work hard. And I know you work hard.'

'I will work hard,' Rocky told her coach.

'And if you are not distracted,' Heracles added, glancing at some of the other girls chatting to some of the men's youth team who were warming up for a training session.

Rocky looked from her teammates to her coach. 'I won't be distracted.'

'Not by social life, maybe,' Heracles mused. 'But as well as having the world at your feet, you seem to me sometimes to have the weight of the world on your shoulders. This is something the British say, yes?'

And it all came back. Mum. Worry about Mum. Dad. Sadness. Ffion. That was why she loved football so much. It made everything you had to worry about disappear.

Rocky didn't reply. She didn't want to burden her football coach with non-football matters.

'I am more than your football coach,' Heracles said. There it was again. Serina Heracles saying things as if she could hear what Rocky was thinking. 'You have a complicated life, no?'

Rocky smiled. 'Home in one box. Football in the other,' she said. 'It's quite simple.'

Rocky was well aware that her coach was offering support and she liked that, she was flattered by it. But she had this thing in her that wanted to shut down any link between football and the rest of her life.

'But home is difficult?' Heracles pressed.

'A bit.'

Serina Heracles nodded. 'I know you have suffered the loss of your father. And I am sorry.'

'Thank you.'

'How is your mother?'

Rocky coughed and smiled. 'Getting there, thanks,' she said.

They were off the pitch now and heading into the corridor where the dressing rooms were and Coach's office. They stopped. The only other sound was the laughing and shouting from the dressing room.

'The drill today?' Coach asked, appearing to change the subject. 'Did you enjoy it?'

Rocky was glad Heracles had changed the subject. Back to football. Safe.

'Very much,' Rocky beamed.

'And you understand now that we tackle not alone? We do it in twos or threes. We need help to win the ball. We cannot do it alone. Not normally?'

'I get that. It was good,' Rocky said.

'I will ask again. How is your mother?' Coach repeated, a slight smile on her face.

And the penny dropped. Rocky, who had

been about to turn away and bury her feelings until she got home, fell silent. Her coach was offering to help her tackle her problems, to support her. And her natural instinct was to reject help, to say she was fine.

'Come into my office,' Serina Heracles said. 'Tell me. I can help you tackle things off the pitch too, perhaps.'

THEY SAT LOOKING at each other across a desk. It was a small room. A desk and chair for Heracles and two chairs the other side of the desk. A whiteboard on the wall, wiped clean. And a set of simple shelves with six box files marked 1 to 6. No words.

Minimalist.

They had been sitting there for less than a minute and Rocky was talking like she'd never talked before. It was very strange. She remembered seeing a film where a woman goes to a priest and confesses her sins, pouring out a lifetime of problems and disasters, how the priest just drew all that pain out of his parishioner. Rocky realised that she revered Heracles so much that she treated her a bit like a priest at a confessional.

She began by explaining how her mum had stopped doing all the things she used to do: shutting windows, turning the heating off, clearing plates, knowing exactly who was playing in what game and at what time. Then she talked about her mum's mood, her drinking alone, the sound of her crying at night.

'And you have taken her to the doctor?' Heracles leaned forward, rubbing the corner of her left eye.

'Yes. They're going to help.'

'Good. And what more can you do?'

Rocky shrugged. 'Be there?' she suggested.

Heracles nodded. 'Look,' she said. 'I have a story. It's maybe the same for you. Maybe not. But I will tell it anyway. When I was younger my father died. My mother was low. We were quite distant from each other, my mother and I. Never close. Not like you and your mum. But still, every winter, we would go to the north of Sweden for a week and have a sauna every night, then sit in the icy weather outside under the stars. Like every year, I did this. And this is when we talked. I told her about my feelings and she told me about hers and this would do for a whole year. We still do it now.'

'That's nice,' Rocky smiled. She could see it was a happy memory for her coach.

'You can try it? Here. You have spa days, yes? Places to go for a sauna and to pamper, yes?'

'Oh... you mean me and Mum doing a spa day?' She felt herself shiver. 'No way. Not me. I don't like stuff like that.'

Serina Heracles put her head to one side and smiled gently.

'But does your mother like stuff like that?'

Rocky shrugged. She felt herself blush. 'I don't know. To be honest.' But then a memory came back. One time when Dad took Rocky and Roy to a match, Mum went to some sort of spa weekend and came back different. All chilled.

'Yes...' Rocky said to her coach. 'I think maybe she does.'

WHEN ROCKY GOT home, Mum was in the front room with the TV news on.

'What are you doing on Saturday, Mum?' Rocky asked.

'Not much,' Mum smiled, stretching. 'I suppose I'll keep an eye on Roy's game on the TV. There's still a chance of the playoffs, isn't there? Might even do some cleaning.'

'Not this Saturday, Mum,' Rocky said, wincing when she remembered that it was the last league game of the season for the men's team this Saturday. But some things were more important than football. She'd booked a spa day. 'I'm taking you on a mystery trip.'

## 12

ROCKY HAD NEVER felt so uncomfortable in her life. Why had she agreed to this stupid idea?

Assailed by relaxing music and uncomfortable with smiling people walking around in fluffy white dressing gowns, she just wanted to bolt to the loo and hide. It was too much.

Rocky Race shuddered.

'Are you okay, love?' Mum asked.

'Yeah,' Rocky said, automatically.

She felt her mum's eyes on her.

Desperate not to appear ill at ease, she did

what she always did to change a conversation she wasn't enjoying.

'They'll be warming up on the pitch now,' Rocky said.

'The men?'

'Yeah.'

Rocky checked the white clock on the wall in reception as they passed through to the changing rooms. It was midday. Half an hour before Melchester Rovers Men played in their last league game of the season. All the games in the Championship today were kicking off at twelve-thirty.

*So what am I doing here?* she asked herself again.

It was a big question. Why was Rocky putting herself through the torture of a spa day when the football team she had followed all her life were playing in a game that – if they won – they might just scrape into the playoffs to get promoted to the Premier League? A game on TV, but still she felt weird not watching it. The answer?

The answer was Mum.

Mum. Mum. Mum.

Today was about Mum. Mum being happy. Mum being the focus of everything. Sometimes football had to come second. And – after Rocky and Roy had realised that Mum was depressed – it felt fine that football should come second.

The stark truth was that four results had to go Melchester's way and that some of them were highly unlikely. Rocky thought gambling was stupid, but she had looked at the odds for all the games to go in Melchester Rovers' favour. If you combined all the odds, there was a 180-1 chance Melchester Rovers would make the playoffs. That just wasn't going to happen.

'Shall we start with a swim?' Mum suggested.

'Yeah,' Rocky nodded. 'That's good.'

Rocky was happy swimming. It was what came after that she was uneasy about. A massage. She wasn't looking forward to that at all. But she'd booked herself and Mum side-by-side massages all the same.

As they were about to head into the women's changing room, on the edge of the pool, a familiar face appeared. Rocky found herself face to face with a man in another fluffy white dressing gown.

'Jimmy?'

Jimmy Slade. In the flesh.

'It's RRRRRRRRRocky? And... oh ... er... hello... Mrs Race.'

'How are you, Jimmy?'

There was a moment of uneasy silence. Then the three of them were smiling, almost laughing, because they were so uncomfortable.

And then Jimmy Slade was chatting, being Jimmy. Funny. Annoying. And – to some – charismatic.

'Fine thanks, Mrs Race.' Jimmy stepped back, quite close to the edge of the pool.

Rocky glanced at his feet. They were in the water that laps at the edge of a pool and escapes down those slats.

'You can call me Kathleen,' Mum said to him.

Rocky could see that Mum liked Jimmy. Within seconds of meeting him they were like old friends. This was typical Jimmy. Everyone liked him. Everyone laughed when he spoke.

Annoying.

'Fine thanks, Kathleen. I've been told to relax, get a massage. So I'm right for the cup final and if we get into the playoffs. I'm not injured, really.'

Mum nodded.

Rocky had yet to speak to Jimmy since the quarter final when he'd taken the ball from Roy, but couldn't help herself.

'And the fact you're banned because you got booked in that last game,' Rocky said, 'so you can't play anyway.'

Jimmy chuckled. 'Yeah, that too,' he whispered, then winked.

'You annoyed me when you took that free kick,' Rocky said.

Jimmy grinned. 'I know. That's why I did it.'

'To annoy me?' Rocky scowled.

'Yeah. I was on the pitch about to let Roy take it, then I thought of you in the stands. Rocky Race will be really cross if I take this kick, I thought. So I did it.'

Rocky heard Mum laugh. Too much. Like what Jimmy Slade was saying was funny.

'It was wrong,' Rocky added, even more furious now.

Jimmy shrugged. 'I scored,' he said, stepping back so that he was right on the edge of the empty pool now. 'We won.'

Rocky started to feel a ripple of anger. The kind that she knew could very quickly become a tsunami. She clenched her fist inside her dressing gown. This spa. All the calm and niceness. And now Jimmy. It was too much.

'Jimmy?' Rocky looked into his sharp blue eyes.

'Yes, Roxanne?' he replied. 'Because that is your full name, isn't it?'

Mum laughed again. Rocky felt the red mist descending.

'Jimmy. Can you swim?' she asked.

Jimmy made a face. A don't-be-ridiculous face. That of course he could.

'I just need to check… is that a yes?'

'Yes. It's a yes,' Jimmy said.

Rocky reached out with the flat of her hand and pushed Jimmy hard. Taken by surprise, the Melchester Men's midfielder was off balance and falling backwards. His face was a picture. Surprise. Horror. Irritation. All of it made Rocky feel good. So good she laughed so hard she felt tears in her eyes as Jimmy struggled to find his feet at the bottom of the pool.

It took him a few seconds to right himself, take his heavy wet gown off and stand up in the pool.

'That was funny, Rocky,' Jimmy said in a deadpan voice.

'Yes, I thought so,' Rocky replied, smiling. 'Come on, Mum.'

\*    \*    \*

AFTER A SWIM, with Jimmy Slade nowhere to be seen, Rocky and Mum headed for their booked massage.

'He's a nice lad,' Mum said.

'No. He's not.'

Mum wasn't listening. 'Is he always that much fun?'

'He's not fun.'

'Do you fancy him?' Mum asked playfully.

Rocky rolled her eyes. 'You really don't know me at all,' she said. Then regretted it.

'What does that mean?' Mum asked.

Rocky smiled and said, 'Nothing. He's not my type, that's all.'

'Right,' Mum said.

They were at the door to the massage room. Rocky pushed it, putting an end to a conversation with her mum about who she didn't fancy and why.

Inside, Rocky had to fight her natural aversion to the gentle music and the sweet smell of some sort of oil that was supposed to make you feel even more relaxed than you were already supposed to be. Even though she felt ever more tense. But she would do this. Do this for her mum.

'Morning, ladies,' one of the two masseuses said. 'Whenever you are ready.'

'That'll be never,' Rocky muttered under her breath.

'Sorry?' the masseuse asked.

'Please ignore my daughter,' Mum said gently. 'She's not big on relaxing. She's doing this for me, so she might not be like your normal client.'

'Understood,' the masseuse said.

And now Rocky felt like crying. That her mum knew she was doing all this to make her happy, that she'd willingly tell that to a stranger. It was nice. Really nice. And that's why she felt like crying.

But she wouldn't cry. She lay down on her front and felt the masseuse arranging towels on top of her, then heard oil or something being squirted out of a bottle. The sound of two oily hands rubbing together.

'Your muscles are very tense,' the masseuse said in a gentle voice after a few seconds of the massage.

'I like them that way,' Rocky said.

'You don't want to relax? Feel more chilled?'

Rocky shook her head, then she eased herself up. 'Do you mind if I just lie here and chat to my mum? I don't really like having massages. Is that okay? I don't want to be rude. It's not you.'

Rocky heard her mum laugh. The masseuse

said it was not a problem, laughing too.

Rocky lay on her side and faced her mum. Mum was having her back rubbed, from the shoulders, down the spine. She was smiling.

'Is that good?' Rocky asked.

'Very good,' Mum smiled.

'Good.'

'How are you feeling about the game tomorrow?' Mum asked.

'Excited,' Rocky said, 'to play against a US team.'

'And to see Ffion?'

'Yeah.'

'Going to America is quite a thing for a girl her age,' Mum said.

Rocky nodded. She was still conflicted about Ffion and what she'd said. Yes, she was excited to see her, but she couldn't stop thinking about her comments. And the fact she had not challenged Ffion.

'Would you ever do that?' Mum asked.

'Do what?' Rocky was confused.

'Go to the States?'

Rocky shook her head, ignoring the fact that it was something she had definitely fantasised about several times. Boarding a plane, landing in the US, joining a team of footballers at a university. How amazing would that be?

'Why not?' Mum asked.

'I can't leave you.' Rocky said it without thinking about how her mum would react. It just came out.

Mum's reaction was surprising. She sat up. The masseuse stepped back.

'Rocky. I need you to listen. Yes, I am a widow. Yes, I am sad. And yes, I have you and Roy. You two are where my happiness comes from. And I get a lot of it. But I will only be happy if you are living your lives in the most fulfilling way you can. If you need to go to play football in the US, then I need you to do that. Do you understand?'

Rocky heard cheering from somewhere else in the spa facility, but ignored it. What her mum had just said. It was game changing. Life changing.

Mum was still talking. About what she was going to do to make herself feel better. She had signed up to volunteer at the local refugee centre and she was training to do a few hours on a family helpline every week. She was busy. Her friends in the Netherlands had invited her to visit.

'Do you promise me?' Mum said at the end of her speech.

'Promise you what?' Rocky had been thinking about going to America. Not that it would really happen. Things like that wouldn't happen. Not to her.

'That you won't hold yourself back because you think you're being kind to me?'

'I...'

'Promise now.'

Rocky sighed. She liked that her mum was like this. Firm. Decisive. Strong.

'I promise,' Rocky agreed.

BACK IN THE pool, Rocky and Mum drifted around in the water. Not swimming. Just chatting and wiggling their legs and arms a bit. It felt nice. Rocky acknowledged that she felt relaxed, just bobbing about in the water, head under the surface, ears covered up. Even so, she thought she heard another cheer. Or chanting. But she assumed it was the way water plays in your ears and makes you hear roaring and booming. And she was too busy thinking about what Mum had said to her and wild ideas of taking her football career away from Melchester and to live the exciting life she dreamed of. She'd not thought about the men's team for hours.

She saw him come from nowhere. Jimmy Slade.

He leaped from the side of the pool, folded his body into a ball, then bombed into the water next to Rocky. A massive wave hit her like a wall. She choked back the water and tried to find the bottom of the pool with her feet.

Now she was faced with Jimmy Slade's wide grin and shining blue eyes.

'Hey up, Roxanne!' he said.

'You idiot,' she said.

He was still grinning. Staring at her. Grinning, grinning, grinning.

'What?' Rocky muttered, really irritated now.

'You've not heard, have you?'

'Heard what?' Rocky was close to losing her temper. 'Really, Jimmy. You are such a…'

'We won. And Dudley Villa and Portdean lost. And Kingsbay drew.'

Rocky stopped frowning.

'What?'

'What indeed,' Jimmy laughed. 'You tell me...'

And now Rocky turned to Mum, who was still blinking at all the water Jimmy had splashed into her eyes.

'Mum.'

'Love?'

'We're in the playoffs. The men's team. To get promoted to the Premier League.'

THEY DROVE BACK into town to the sound of car horns going off and red and yellow flags streaming out of the back of cars. The city was celebrating sneaking into the playoffs and the chance of promotion to the Premier League.

'This is so cool,' Rocky said to her mum. 'Just look!'

Mum nodded.

'I agree,' she said. 'I wish – and I am saying this without getting maudlin – but I wish your dad could have seen it. His team, our team, on the verge of being back in the top flight. It's lovely. He'd have been happy today.'

'Yes,' Rocky forced a smile.

'So I'm going to be happy too,' Mum said. 'Today… I am happy!'

Rocky couldn't not grin. Mum was more Mum-like. The spa day had worked. Even if it was just for a short time that she felt good, that was a start. They'd just have to go to the spa again. Ideally when Jimmy Slade was not there.

'Are you going to go out and celebrate?' Mum asked.

Rocky shook her head. 'Game tomorrow. I'll let Roy do all that. But I bet he wants an early night.'

They both laughed.

But Rocky felt an unease coming over her now. A sense that there was more to tackle than the game tomorrow. To play against

Steinbeck University was one thing. An honour. She could hardly believe she would be toe to toe with a US football team.

Or soccer team, as they preferred.

But to see Ffion and deal with what she'd said. That was another. Rocky was nervous. She was so excited to see her friend. But she also wanted to tell her how she felt about what Ffion had said about footballers being foreign and white and all that. How did you do that? Did you even do it at all? Wasn't it better just to let it go and hope that your friend realised they had said something racist?

Rocky sighed.

Mum shifted the car up a gear as they drove past Mel Park. Nearly home.

'You can talk to me about your problem today,' Mum said gently. 'I can cope with it today.'

211

'What problem?' Rocky answered defensively.

'I don't know what it is, love. But I know it's there. Eating away at you. Come on. Tell me. Make me feel like a proper mum again.'

Rocky rolled her eyes. 'Do you have to say things like that? You are a proper mum. You always will be.'

Mum smiled. 'Sorry. But, come on. Open up to me.'

Rocky took a deep breath. Right. She'd tell Mum. It was the correct thing to do. It would help her get her thoughts straight. It was good to talk to people and work your thoughts out. So she spilled everything.

'So... I was talking to Ffion on FaceTime and she was making out like Melchester Rovers Women is a team full of foreigners and I think she meant it because we have such diverse backgrounds. And I don't care where our players come from, but the truth is, apart from Yamile, we're all British. Not that it matters. But she was making out like we weren't all British and that – she sort of implied – that you had to be white to be British and then... and then she said that there were only two foreign players in the Steinbeck University team and what she

213

really meant was Black players and she didn't even include herself as foreign in that team...'

'Because she's white?' Mum interrupted.

Rocky nodded. 'But she is foreign. In America she's as foreign as anyone. And I don't know what to say to her, but I really feel like I have to say something.'

The car had stopped. They were home. They sat in silence, side by side, the car air freshener still swinging between them.

'Okay,' Mum said. 'First of all, I am proud of you. You've identified something wrong and you want to challenge it.'

'But should I challenge it?'

'Yes. Yes, of course,' Mum said.

'But how?'

Mum shrugged. 'Just say what you've said to me. Make her aware that you are still friends, that you still love her, but that you want to question something she has said. It doesn't need to be the end of the world. It can be the beginning of a better world.'

Rocky knew her mum was right, but she still felt anxious. She could feel a wave of panic rippling through her body. And she so didn't want to start all that panic stuff again. She hoped that was behind her.

'But when? As soon as I see her? Even before we play the game?'

'When it seems right,' Mum said. 'Maybe after the game if you're both wound up pre-match. I don't know. But make sure you find the time.'

'Okay.' Rocky was aware her voice sounded small.

'It's the right thing to do,' Mum said. 'It might feel horrible, but it's the right thing. And it doesn't mean you're some hero either. It's just something that needs saying.'

'Yeah,' Rocky said. 'Thanks, Mum.'

WHEN ROCKY SAW Ffion climbing off the Steinbeck University coach outside Mel Park, she couldn't help but run and throw herself at her friend, her hero. Grabbing her, she pulled her into a hug and wouldn't let go as Ffion's teammates laughed and joked about the warm welcome Ffion was getting.

'I missed you,' Rocky said. She felt overjoyed. It had been too long since they'd seen each other. Far too long.

Ffion nodded. She looked more serious than overjoyed.

'What is it?' Rocky asked. 'Is everything

okay? Is it your mum or dad? You look upset.'

Ffion nodded. 'Yeah. No one is ill or anything. We just need to talk.'

Rocky noticed the other women in the Steinbeck University team were watching, as if waiting for Ffion to tell them what to do.

'You carry on. I just need to sort something with Rocky,' Ffion told them. Then Ffion put her arm around Rocky's shoulder and – together – they walked through the large stadium entrance at the corner of Mel Park. They walked in silence, until Ffion broke the spell.

'Good to be back here,' Ffion mused, gazing into the backs of the stands.

'Do you miss it?' Rocky asked.

'I only miss people,' Ffion said. 'You. Mum. Vic. And Roy.'

'Right,' Rocky said.

218

The tension between them was visible in their faces. They were staring at each other. Under the floodlights. Not smiling. But no aggression. Just confusion.

'Look,' Rocky took a deep breath. 'I have to say something.'

'Okay...' Ffion said.

'What you said about... I'm not sure...' Rocky felt rubbish. How did you tell someone you looked up to so much that they had got something wrong?

'Just say it, Rocky.'

'Okay. Okay. Well... when we were talking about our teams' players you said that my teammates with names like Danquah and Pielichaty and Aluko didn't sound British, but they are British. Like we're British.'

Ffion opened her mouth to speak. But Rocky held up her hand to silence her. She had what she wanted to say clear in her mind and needed to get it out. To articulate how she felt.

'Then you said that your team had only two foreigners. One from Ghana. One from Mexico. And you said that the rest of you were not foreign and you meant that the rest of you were white and then you didn't say that you are foreign in America and it felt

like – to me – that you meant the rest of you were white and that to be foreign means you are not white or have a different-sounding name to something like Race or Guthrie.

'And I wanted to tell you how I felt because it made me feel uncomfortable and I wanted you to know that you – who I care… who I love… needed to know you'd said something that made me feel like that.'

Rocky felt exhausted. She could barely remember feeling so exhausted. The energy that had taken! But she felt that she had had to do it.

Now it was Ffion's turn to speak.

'I have been thinking about it too,' she said in a quiet voice. 'After we got cut off. Did you kill the call?'

Rocky nodded. 'Yeah.'

'Okay.' Ffion took a deep breath now. 'I wanted to say you were right. And I was wrong. Right to question what I said about players and where they come from. And I was wrong to say what I said about who was British and who wasn't. And that I was wrong when I said that my teammates were foreign, but that I wasn't. And I wanted to say that I have no excuses. It was racist. I was racist. And that I am truly sorry.'

Rocky nodded, then she saw two figures jogging down the side of the pitch, having emerged from the players' tunnel. Two men.

Ffion had her back to them. But Rocky could see who they were. And she knew she wouldn't have Ffion's attention for long.

'That's good to hear,' Rocky said, looking over Ffion's shoulder. 'You've two visitors. We can talk later if you want to?'

'I do,' Ffion said. 'I'm sorry.'

Then the players from the men's team arrived.

Ffion hugged her brother, Vic, first, Roy standing at a distance until they'd done. Then she hugged Roy. All this as Rocky felt a massive sense of elation and relief. She hadn't needed to push it. Ffion got what had bothered her.

Rocky smiled to herself that Roy was so uneasy. But she felt sorry for him too. He loved Ffion. He missed her. It was sad they were finished. But she was living her dream and it was better to do the right thing than not, just because you're worried someone will be sad.

Rocky was glad to put all the non-football things in their box and pull on her Melchester Rovers strip to play.

Thinking football. Only football.

The game was very different to what Rocky

was used to playing in. There was something about the way Steinbeck University played that mesmerised her.

It was all about possession. Keeping the ball, moving forward, trying to break down the Melchester defence. It was class. It was control. It was awesome.

But Rocky had been tasked to stop it. By her coach.

'They will play with the ball all the time. Like Barcelona Men at their best. Or Spain when they used to win tournaments. Pass. Pass. Pass. Run off the ball. Pass. It is, for me, boring,' Serina Heracles laughed as she started to bring her team talk to an end.

'Rocky, you must play deep. In front of the defence. Break up the play. You are the anti-footballer today. And press. All the time, press. All of you. Create pressure on them so they pass it back. We must frustrate them.

Then they will take more risks. This is how we trained and now it is how we must play.

'Also, respect them, don't fear them. You must not fear them just because they are American and American teams are better that European teams. Think also that they will expect to beat us. They don't so much want to beat us. They expect it. This, you must use to steel yourselves.'

Rocky led her team out alongside Ffion, who was captaining Steinbeck University. She could not help but think about what Heracles had said to her.

*Think also that they will expect to beat us.*

*They don't so much want to beat us.*

*They expect it.*

How annoying was that? There was no way Rocky was going to let that happen. And there was something Rocky liked about being called an anti-footballer too. To destroy the game. Negate it. Unpick it. Yes, she could do that.

And then the game began. Rocky pressed, closed down, tackled, blocked, trying to make the way the American team played as ugly as possible.

And yet, it was hard not to be distracted by the athleticism of the US players, by their fitness and flexibility, their team system. But Rocky managed to focus. She worked out quickly that the Americans played with a pivot in the midfield, who took the ball with her back to the goal she was attacking, then sprayed passes out to the left and right or drew a foul.

The first time the pivot took the ball, Rocky was onto her, clean-tackling as she tried to play the ball wide. Then again. There was a fixed nature to the way the Americans played. Keeping the ball across the defence and deep midfield, then getting the ball to the pivot and wide-played running into three or four positions, potentially ripping the Melchester defence to ribbons.

Rocky didn't give the pivot time. She didn't close mark her. But she stayed within ten metres of her all the time, waiting for the ball to be played into her. She was so glad she had been practising on the Terrible 200, the steep steps on the edge of the Moor that Roy had taught her to run up to build her stamina. The repeated fast runs would be shattering her now if she hadn't. More and more, Rocky tackled her, blocked her passes, panicked her into spraying a loose ball into touch.

Just after half time, Rocky went in again hard and this time the Pivot's arm came out and bashed Rocky on the nose.

A sharp sting of pain. Unable to see, Rocky went down.

It was a clear foul. She could hear shouting and the sound of one of her teammates fronting up to the pivot. The ref separating them.

As her vision came back, Rocky couldn't believe what she was seeing.

Ffion was standing over her teammate, the pivot, having clearly pushed her to the ground. And the ref – after showing Ffion a yellow – was showing the red to the pivot.

'It wasn't that bad,' Rocky said, trying to get up, a searing pain across her nose. 'Not a red.'

'Don't argue with me or you'll get a yellow like this one,' the ref said. 'She's walking.'

Rocky caught the pivot giving her a dark look as she stormed off the pitch. Normally she loved nothing more than getting an opponent sent off. But Rocky felt bad for the American. Here she was in a country miles away from home and she'd been ordered off. She'd come a long way. For what? Rocky almost felt like she'd been a bad host going down. But she'd not dived. It had been genuine. The pain testified to that.

Still 0–0.

But with the extra player, Rocky felt like they had a chance with no more than forty minutes to go.

'Keep the shape. The same game plan,' Heracles shouted from the touchline.

But as the game went on – even with an extra player – the American team's fitness and athleticism were beginning to show. They were forcing Melchester Rovers deeper and deeper.

Another attack late in the game. Still 0–0. Just six minutes left. The ball played wide to Ffion in Steinbeck University blue. Ffion chose to run hard at the Melchester defence this time. It was good to see. This was like the Ffion of old, adventurous, an individual, not part of a system that, although effective, seemed too fixed, too frustrating for her flair.

Ffion fought past Eve Ainsworth and Emma Aluko. And suddenly she was one-on-one with Lily Halifax in the Melchester net as Rocky thundered towards her, giving it everything. There was no way she would let Ffion score. No way. Rocky saw her touch the ball once, then again, her next touch would be a strike, from twelve yards out, Lily Halifax closing the angles, but the goal seemed huge. Rocky had to get a foot on it. She lunged, pointing her foot, sliding in, making contact, clipping the ball away from Ffion's certain goal. This had to be the tackle of her life so far.

And it was. The perfect tackle. Except…

Except Rocky's perfect tackle had taken the ball beyond Lily Halifax, onto the left-hand post and… into the net.

Rocky heard the roar of celebration from the US players.

And she knew.

Rocky had scored.

An own goal.

She lay on the ground and put her head in her hands. Swore under her breath.

Then a voice. A shout from the stands. 'Come on, Rocky! On your feet!'

Rocky searched among the fans packing the main stand.

Still on the ground, her eyes locked onto her mum's. She'd had no idea Mum was here. She had come to a game for the first time in ages – the first time since Dad died – and it was wonderful to see.

Rocky glanced at the stadium clock. Five minutes left. At least. Plenty of time. She jumped to her feet and ran into the goal, grabbed the ball and jogged back to the centre circle, acknowledging Mum who she could see was sitting with Roy and Vic and some of the men's team.

Several of her teammates hit her on the back.

'Unlucky.'

'It was going to be a goal anyway.'

'Don't worry.'

That's what they were saying.

Rocky nodded, placed the ball on the centre spot and stood on it, glaring at the referee, encouraging her to make the US team players stop running around with their arms in the air. They were celebrating like they'd won the league or something.

Annoying. Very.

Melchester Rovers 0 Steinbeck University 1.

Five minutes to go.

Rocky closed her eyes when the final whistle went. She put her hands on her knees and sighed. She was shattered. She'd given it everything. It was over.

'Damn it,' she said to the mud under her feet.

Then Ffion was there. With two of the other Steinbeck University players. There were lots of pats on the back, handshakes. It seemed half the team were wanting to talk to Rocky.

'Don't beat yourself up about the goal.'

'You were immense.'

'Big respect.'

'Player of the match.'

Rocky smiled, said thank you and watched as Ffion jogged over to see Mum, hugging her in the front row of the stand after climbing over the advertising hoardings.

A nice touch.

Rocky walked over to join them. Mum gave her a hug.

'I'm so proud of you, love,' Mum said.

'Thanks, Mum. Proud of me for scoring an own goal?'

Mum laughed. 'For you and your football. You were the best player on the pitch. No doubt. I can see why they want you.'

Rocky had no idea what Mum was talking about. Why who wanted her? Melchester? Well, she knew that. She understood she was a big part of the team and – well – she was captain, wasn't she?

'I'll see you at home, Mum. I won't be long.'

Mum smiled and waved, and Rocky joined Ffion who was waiting for her. She felt another rush of happiness. It was good to see Mum out and about, not in the front room looking miserable. Her mum had said she'd fight back against grief and she was. Rocky was proud of her.

'So listen…' Ffion said to Rocky as they walked to the tunnel, the last players to leave the pitch.

'What?'

'My coach has asked me to ask you something.'

'Right,' Rocky said. 'About what?'

'About you.'

Rocky stopped walking. Ffion too. They were standing in a mostly empty stadium now. The noise of cars on the streets outside rumbling. A plane overhead.

Rocky didn't say anything. But she remembered Mum's words. *I can see why they want you.*

'I talked to your mum about it. Coach wanted me to ask your mum before I ask you.'

'Ask me what?' Rocky felt suddenly panicked. What was this?

'And your mum thinks it's amazing.'

'You've lost me.'

'My coach wants you to come to the States. On a scholarship. To study at the university and to play for us.'

'I can't.' It came out without Rocky even thinking it through. A reflex. *No. I can't. I won't.*

'Why not?' Ffion asked.

'Mum.'

'Your mum says you can.'

Rocky shook her head. 'No.'

'I told her,' Ffion insisted. 'I asked her first.

I asked her if we can ask you. She said we must. She said this is a great opportunity for you. That she loves you and that she knows it is what you really want.'

Rocky shook her head.

'No,' she said.


ROY GAVE ROCKY a lift home.

'You were immense today,' he said.

'Thanks.' Rocky knew she sounded glum.

'You still annoyed by the OG?'

'Not really.'

'Are you sure?'

'No. Look, I did my best. I was unlucky. She would have scored anyway. In the end it was me score or she scores... Maybe I should have let her. It would have felt good to come back here and score the winner. Show us that she's the legend we remember.'

'Good attitude,' Roy smiled, as he changed gear and they approached a roundabout.

'So, did Ffion tell you?'

'Did Ffion tell me what?' Roy asked.

'About the offer of a scholarship.'

'No. Who for? Hang on… for you?'

'Yeah, me.' Rocky sat deep into the passenger seat of her brother's car. She felt small. She felt like she wanted to sink into the seat. Hide.

'That's amazing, Rocky,' Roy said as they turned right and up the hill to their street. 'Is it for real?'

'Yeah.'

Roy was quiet for a moment. 'And you're not sure?'

'That's right, yeah.' Rocky could feel she was slipping into herself. This was too much.

More silence.

Roy parked outside their house and Rocky put her hand out to open the passenger door.

'Wait,' Roy said.

Rocky waited and stared at the small terraced house on the hill on the side of Melchester where she had always lived. Today it looked different. She knew why. Her world was suddenly bigger. Or it could be. If she chose for it to be bigger. But she couldn't let that happen. She had to stay for Mum. Didn't she?

Then Roy was talking.

'Do you remember when I walked you to school that day – three, four years ago – and you asked for my help in finding a football team and you said it wasn't fair that I had opportunities to play proper football and you didn't?'

Rocky nodded. *Here we go*, she thought. *I can read his next move like he's telegraphed it.*

'Well, you're right,' Roy went on. 'There are fewer opportunities for women to play elite football. But you're getting one.'

'I can't...'

'Why not?'

'Mum!' Rocky shouted suddenly. 'She lost Dad. She's depressed.'

Roy shook his head. 'If she thinks for a minute you are not going to do this because of her, she'll be more than depressed. And, anyway, she's getting help now. She's got plans.'

'She needs us.'

'And she's got us. Me here and you there. I'm not moving out. I like living with Mum.'

'But she needs me.'

Roy was shaking his head. And the annoying thing was she knew he was right and she was wrong.

'Rocky, don't you get what being a mum

is?' he argued. 'She lives through her children. When we do well, she feels like she has done well. When we smile, she smiles. When we travel the world playing football, living the dream, she lives the dream. You want her to be happy?'

'Course I do,' Rocky grumbled.

'Then you have to make yourself happy,' Roy said.

Rocky sat alone in her bedroom for an hour, staring at the back of the door where she used to have a mirror, but that she had removed because… she couldn't remember.

Leaning back against the headboard of her bed she frowned and surveyed the pile of her old school books.

Redundant now.

She looked at posters of bands that were still up on the wall, but they were bands she hadn't liked for years. And she had this sense that this bedroom wasn't hers. That it was someone else's.

Whose?

Well, it was hers of course.

The bedroom she had slept in pretty much every night of her life.

And she knew that it was over.

Her childhood.

Done.

Melchester.

Done.

Rocky Race stood up, took a deep breath, then sighed.

This was it then.

The big moment. The end. Or was it a beginning?

Downstairs, Mum was in the kitchen baking a cake.

Rocky frowned. 'Bit late for baking, isn't it, Mum?'

'I have to make this,' Mum said. Her eyes were red.

'Why? Who's it for?' Rocky asked, sensing Roy behind her.

'You,' Mum said. 'It's to celebrate.'

Rocky nodded. 'What's to celebrate?'

'So you're not going to accept the offer?' Mum asked.

Rocky looked at the kitchen. The pots they kept tea and coffee in. The sugar bowl. The kettle. All the things in the kitchen. Like the things in her bedroom, they looked different today.

Things were different. Things had changed. And they would go on changing. It was the only way. It was good. Even if part of her felt bad about it.

'No. I'm going to accept. I'm going to say yes.'

# Thank you

I'd like to say a big thank you to the several people who have helped me write *Game Changer*.

Simon Robinson is very a good friend of mine. Since I started writing the *Roy of the Rovers* books, Simon has been a huge support, challenging me to make these books as good as I can make them. Thank you, Simon.

Olivia Hicks and Amy Borsuk have worked tirelessly as my editors. Their ideas and guidance – and enthusiasm for Rocky – have been a huge boost. Thank you, Amy and Olivia.

Thanks too, to Rob Williams who writes the Roy of the Rovers graphic novels. We dovetail our books and some of the very best ideas that I have written in this series came from him. Great storyteller.

Finally, thank you to my daughter. Conversations we've had over the last couple of years have really helped me with this book.

Some of Rocky's teammates are named after writers who are currently writing fiction about football. They include Helena Pielichaty, Eve Ainsworth, Narinder Dhami, Priscilla Mante and Yamile Mendez. Also, one other team mate is named after Eniola Aluko, whose autobiography – *They Don't Teach This* – is fantastic.

Please check out their books and support them like you would your favourite football team at your local library or bookshop. They're all great.

# THE STORY CONTINUES!

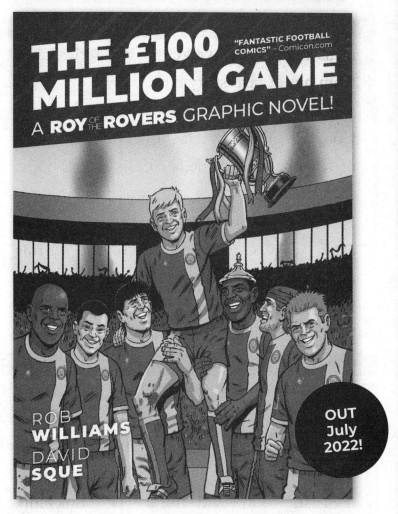

It's the thrilling conclusion of the third season of *Roy of the Rovers!* Roy and the Melchester Rovers have survived heartache and hurdles on the field and off. Now, with the final of the premiership cup looming, another crisis at home threatens to knock Roy off his game...

For more **ROY OF THE ROVERS** find us online:

# www.royoftherovers.com

# SEASON 1

# S E A S O N  2

## ILLUSTRATED FICTION

### ON TOUR
Author: Tom Palmer
Illustrator: Dan Cornwell
ISBN: 978-1-78108-685-8

**READ?** ☐

### FROM THE ASHES
Author: Tom Palmer
Illustrator: Dan Cornwell
ISBN: 978-1-78108-783-1

**READ?** ☐

### ROCKY
Author: Tom Palmer
Illustrator: Dan Cornwell
ISBN: 978-1-78108-826-5

**READ?** ☐

## GRAPHIC NOVELS

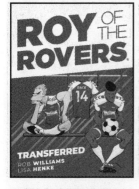

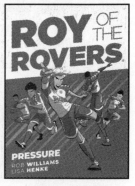

### TRANSFERRED
Writer: Rob Williams
Artist: Lisa Henke
ISBN: 978-1-78108-750-3

**READ?** ☐

### ALL TO PLAY FOR
Writer: Rob Williams
Artist: Lisa Henke
ISBN: 978-1-78108-756-5

**READ?** ☐

### PRESSURE
Writer: Rob Williams
Artist: Lisa Henke
ISBN: 978-1-78108-764-0

**READ?** ☐

# SUPPORT YOUR CHILD'S READING SKILLS
## THROUGH FOOTBALL

### FOR PARENTS

Here are some top tips to get your kids excited about reading and writing using the power of football!

### Become a football detective

Challenge your child to find out as much as they can about their favourite footballer: their age, their best goal celebration – even their most famous haircut! Encourage them to find out fun facts about their favourite player by searching for information online, reading football magazines and visiting the library.

### It's ok to substitute a book that isn't match fit

Don't force your child to finish a book they aren't enjoying. Go to your local library and let your child try out lots of different styles and ways of reading – from autobiographies and audiobooks, to novels and ebooks.

### Turn reading into a team effort

Reading together with your child, even after they can read for themselves, helps you bond, share stories together and shows your child that stories are important, powerful and – above all – fun!

### Write your way into football history

Football is filled with magical moments, difficult decisions, opinions and statistics. After a big game, help your child use their love of football to write a match report, a blog (lots of top ballers have these), a newspaper article or a script for an online video about what happened.

### Don't show reading the red card

All types of reading counts, so if your child enjoys reading online, reading comics, graphic novels, magazines, as well as books, that's good too! Ask your child's teacher or your local library for recommendations that will get your child excited about reading.

### Support Team Reading!

Donate to the National Literacy Trust to give the gift of reading. Visit **literacytrust.org.uk/donate** to support their work in the UK's most disadvantaged communities, working with families and children to raise literacy levels giving them the skills they need to succeed.

**National Literacy Trust**

Changing life stories

Visit wordsforlife.org.uk for more family reading and writing activities

Registered charity no. 1116260 (England and Wales) and SC042944 (Scotland)

# FINISHED READING THIS COMIC?
## WHAT CAN YOU DO NEXT?

**FOR KIDS**

Discover ways your love of football can help you improve your skills in class

### What happens next?

Why not continue the story of this book once you've finished it? Try and write an extra chapter about what you think the characters do next.

### Write a review of this book to share with your friends ★ ★ ★

What did you think of this book? How many stars out of five would you give the plot and why? Put on your thinking cap and write a short review of what you have read so your friends can see what you particularly liked about it.

### Share the story with your family

Take to the living room stage and try reading this book out loud to someone at home. It's a great way to practise your reading – and acting! Remember to speak nice and clearly.

### Create your own comic strip

What's your favourite part of football? The songs, the teamwork or maybe even the team talks? Pick something you love about football and create your own story in a comic strip.

### Write a thank you letter ✉

Show the person who bought you this book how much you appreciate the gift and write them a thank you letter. You can practise your best professional autograph at the end of it too!

### Keepy uppy with your reading

Visit your local library to explore all kinds of different sporting magazines and books if you've found this one interesting.

**National Literacy Trust**

Changing life stories

**Visit wordsforlife.org.uk for more family reading and writing activities**

# YOUR REVIEWS MATTER!

Enjoy this book? Got something to say?
Leave a review on Amazon, GoodReads or with your
favourite bookseller and let the world know!